EAST YORKSHIRE
FOLK
TALES

EAST YORKSHIRE

FOLK TALES

INGRID BARTON

The
History
Press

First published 2015

The History Press
The Mill, Brimscombe Port
Stroud, Gloucestershire, GL5 2QG
www.thehistorypress.co.uk

Reprinted 2017

British Library Cataloguing in Publication Data.
A catalogue record for this book is available from the British Library.

ISBN 978 0 7524 9445 6

Typesetting and origination by The History Press
Printed in Great Britain

All images by the author

CONTENTS

ACKNOWLEDGEMENTS

I would like to thank all my supportive friends, including Dr Charles Kightly and my partner Chris, who was forced to listen to me telling the stories.

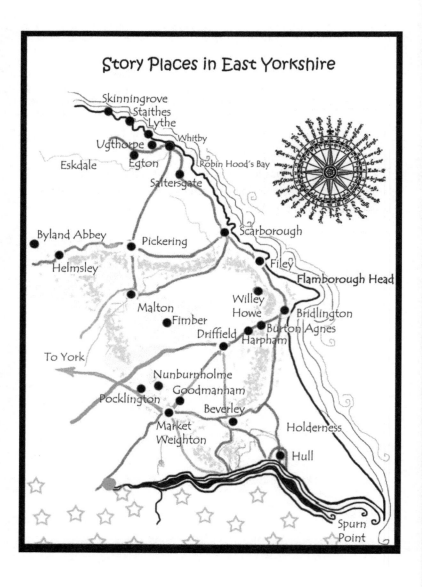

Story Places in East Yorkshire

ABOUT THE AUTHOR

INGRID BARTON is an experienced oral storyteller and former director of the Society for Storytelling, with a life-long interest in folklore, archaeology and the oral tradition. She is the author of *North Yorkshire Folk Tales* and lives in Kilnwick Percy in the East Riding.

INTRODUCTION

Yorkshire is a huge county that, like Caesar's Gaul, was once divided into three parts (Thridings → Thirdings → Ridings). The traditional ridings were eliminated in one of the twentieth century's infamous boundary changes, but though there is once again an East Riding of Yorkshire – an heroic tale in itself – I have chosen to include stories from the whole East Yorkshire coastal strip (parts of which are now technically in North Yorkshire), as they seem to belong together. If you have read *North Yorkshire Folk Tales* and missed tales from Whitby or Scarborough, you will find them here.

East Yorkshire has borne the brunt of a lot of English history: Anglo-Saxon and Viking invasions, the Harrying of the North, the Pilgrimage of Grace, press gangs, pirates and the Luftwaffe. Its people are tough, unsentimental and independent, its stories downbeat and unromantic, often with a sly, bubble-pricking humour.

As readers may be more familiar with York and the Dales, a very brief description of East Yorkshire might be useful. First there are the Wolds, high areas of chalk, similar to the South Downs. It was mostly rough grazing until the nineteenth century, so there are few villages and even fewer traditional stories, though the landscape is full of prehistoric burial mounds and dykes.

To the south-east of the Wolds is Holderness, flat, rich, agricultural land, much of which has been reclaimed from the huge Humber Estuary. It includes Spurn Point at the mouth of the Humber, ever-changing as storms and the laying down of river silt modify its shape.

The east coast, which stretches from the Humber up to the Tees, was once a place of little fishing villages (with some alum mining near Whitby), but its inhabitants have mostly given up the struggle of making a living from fish and now rely on a healthy tourist industry which exploits their stormy smuggling past.

NB: Translations of the Anglo-Saxon verses and the illustrations were done by myself.

Ingrid Barton, 2015

1

ANIMALS

How Filey Got its Brig

Filey
The seaside town of Filey once straddled the boundaries of the
East and North Ridings. They joined at the edge of a small ravine.
The church at the top of the north side was in the North Riding
and the town to the south in the East Riding. (It was a local joke
to say that someone had moved to the North Riding when they
had, in fact, died.) It must have been in this very gully that the
dragon in the following story lived.

Once there was a dragon who lived in a deep ravine in Filey.
Few people cared to live anywhere near him except an old
woman, Mrs Greenaway, who inhabited a cottage in the
woods above. She was what people called a 'gifted' woman –
a white witch – so the dragon didn't bother her, even though
he was becoming hungrier and hungrier all the time because
the local farmers had moved their sheep a long way back from
the sea coast so that he couldn't get them.

On the other side of the ravine lived Billy Biter. He was a
travelling tailor. When his mother had been alive, his little
cottage had been the most welcoming in the area, with a kettle

on the boil over a good fire, old Tom Puss washing himself in the chimney corner, and a warm welcome for anyone who cared to drop in for a gossip. In those days folk would fetch water and chop logs for Mrs Biter when Billy was away on his tailoring work, and Mrs Greenaway kept an eye on her as well.

But when Mrs Biter died everything changed for the worse.

Poor old Billy! He didn't have time to cook or keep house for himself – even if his mother had bothered teaching him. He was run off his little legs with work, travelling to farms and big houses making clothes for weddings or funerals. Coming home to the cold dark cottage made him miserable; he missed his mum more and more.

In those days there was only one sure solution recommended for improving this state of affairs: marriage. Encouraged by his neighbours, Billy, whose knowledge of women was decidedly limited, jumped into the matrimonial state with both feet, and his eyes shut. He married the first woman who would have him: Hepzibah. She was six foot if she was an inch, broad in the beam as a Filey coble and the village drunk to boot. She was a mean, slovenly, bullying sort of woman; a slattern who always carried a huge tarred leather mug called a blackjack, which could be used for hitting people as well as holding gin or beer or whatever she could get. If Billy had expected her to turn magically into his mother, one week of living with her must have taught him his mistake. No food, no fire, just a great lump of a wife sprawled out drunk over the threshold.

Folk were sorry, of course, because Billy was well liked. 'I reckon Hepzibah married 'im because his cottage is only half a mile from t'pub,' they said, shaking their heads. Too late to warn him now and anyway none of them was up for interfering: they feared the blackjack!

Every day Hepzibah would stagger down the hill to the pub, and every evening Billy would came home to a cold and cheerless house. He would then have to chop firewood and light the fire to boil water. He'd have a bit of a sweep around while old Tom Puss had a few minutes warm in the chimney corner and then he'd fetch the wheelbarrow and go to look for his wife. He'd find her somewhere on the path, asleep on the ground with the blackjack empty next to her. She was a big weight for a tired little man to push back up the hill, but it was just as bad if she actually made it home because she would fall asleep in Billy's mother's old chair, skirt up round her knees, drool coming out of her mouth, and Billy would have to tiptoe around trying not to wake her. He and Tom Puss, who also kept a watchful eye on her, knew that if she woke up she'd most likely be after them both with the broom, and she could run – even when drunk – much faster than Billy with his weak little tailor's legs. On those nights they'd be out of the door and up on the roof faster than you could say 'misery' as soon as they saw her stirring.

One cold windy night, old Mrs Greenaway was in her little house in the wood, looking out of her window, when she saw Billy and Tom Puss up on the roof, huddling around the chimney pot for warmth. She shook her head. (Down in the gully the dragon gave a great groan of hunger, though he didn't stir out.)

The next night was the same. Hepzibah was sprawled over the threshold this time, so, rather than risk stepping over her, Billy and Tom Puss went up on to the roof and sat there in the rain. Mrs Greenaway frowned. (The dragon groaned again, louder this time; a great groan that shook the ground.)

On the third night – it was a cold foggy one – the folk at the farm where Billy was making clothes gave him a good Yorkshire tea and he put a bit in his pocket for Puss. The farmer's wife, seeing him with a face as long as a fiddle, felt sorry for him because he'd always been such a merry little soul who sang at his work, laughed often and danced well, so she made him up a nice pack of food to take home. The famer bound a dry faggot of wood on top to save him work when he got home.

'If Hepzibah can't be bothered to cook, tha'll have to find time to do it thasen,' said the farmer. 'So think on, lad. Now, the pack's a bit heavy, but still it's lighter than the wheelbarrow, eh?'

Billy thanked them and, with the pack on his back, trudged off into the fog, wondering with dread what sort of mood Hepzibah would be in. Her kind moments were just as alarming as her angry ones. She would take him on her knee and bounce him like a baby, saying that he was her darling little man, and giving him beery kisses.

Billy was thinking about this when he smelt the most delicious smell wafting through the trees (he was walking through Mrs Greenaway's wood at the time). The smell was so rich and sweet that he found himself drawn out of his way, right up to her door.

'Come in! Come in! Billy Biter,' she said, 'you and your pack. Hepzibah wouldn't be wanting them. Hand them over.'

This was a bit of a surprise, but she'd been kind to his mother and she was old herself, so he handed over the pack, thinking with regret of the food in it. Mrs Greenaway didn't open it though, she just shook something like flour over it and put it down on the floor of the kitchen.

'I've been baking. Can you smell my parkin? I'll give you a mouthful to warm your way home.' She cut a huge slice from the big square parkin on the hearth (Oh! That smell!) and gave it to him. Down in the gully the dragon smelt it too, and roared.

'Now here's a bit for Tom Puss as well. Look, I'll wrap it up in clean leaves. And this bit HERE – this bit is for Hepzibah – only Hepzibah, mind you, no one else. I'll put it in your pack. Now off you go and sleep well tonight.'

Billy went off, full of good food, with his own slice of parkin warming his hands. He fell into a happy dream, imagining that Hepzibah might have decided to cook a hot meal for once. This pleasant fantasy so occupied his mind that he mistook his way in the fog and stepped right over the edge of the dragon's gully. Down he fell arsey-versey, almost down the dragon's throat. He landed on his pack, which was just as well because the ground was red-hot where the dragon had been grumbling and roaring. When he looked up there was a big round red light next to him. It blinked.

'THAT'S MY EYE YOU'RE POKING YOUR WOOD INTO!' said the dragon. 'LET'S HAVE A LOOK AT YOU. I ALWAYS LIKE TO SEE WHAT I'M EATING!' The dragon squirmed around, sniffing poor Billy, who dropped his slice of parkin and put up his hands to ward him off.

'WHAT'S THAT?' Out of the dragon's mouth came a huge, long, hot, red tongue and gallolloped up the parkin. It stuck delightfully to his teeth, and the taste made his scales rattle with pleasure.

'EEAH!' said the dragon, dropping sticky saliva all over Billy. 'WHAT DO YOU CALL THAT?

'P-p-parkin!' Billy was still lying on his back like a big beetle. He could smell the wood of the faggot beginning to char.

'P-P-PARKIN? GET ME MORE! I MUST HAVE MORE!' At that very moment a crumb of parkin tickled the dragon's nose and he sneezed so hard that he blew Billy clean out of the ravine and right on to the top of his own roof, giving Tom Puss a nasty shock. Billy grabbed the chimney pot for balance, but as he did so the charred rope that held his pack broke. Down the chimney tumbled all the food and the faggot as well, landing on the dying ashes of the fire. It narrowly missed the head of Hepzibah who was snoring on the hearth, her shoelaces undone, her greasy skirts all anyhow and her great blackjack still clutched in

her hand. The smell of the parkin floated delightfully through the house. It floated up the nose of Hepzibah and her red-rimmed eyes opened. What was that? She hauled herself up and looked around. Stuff had fallen down the chimney. There lay a great big slice of parkin, the one Mrs Greenaway had said was specially for her, its leaf wrappings gaping temptingly open! She grabbed it and stuffed it into her mouth. How delicious it was!

The faggot in the ashes began to crackle and burn up brightly. In its light Hepzibah saw the parcel of food and hauled it out. She stared blankly at it. Where had it come from? Then the penny dropped and she shouted up the flue 'You come down here, Billy! I know you're up there! What do you mean by throwing cake at your poor wife? – What sort of cake is it, anyway?'

Billy came down from the roof carefully, but not Tom Puss: he knew when he was well off.

'It's p-parkin. Mrs Greenaway made it.'

'Parkin!' screamed Hepzibah. 'You let another woman cook you parkin! I'll give you parkin, you limp little excuse for a man! What does that old witch know about making parkin? Make parkin for my husband, will she? I'll show her! Get out the pig trough!'

Billy dragged the old pig trough into the house, terrified of what might happen next. However, after his accidental trip to the dragon's gully he was so dazed that he did all Hepzibah demanded in a sort of dream. She took a big bag of oatmeal from the storeroom and emptied it all into the trough. Then she rummaged around, knocking things hither and thither, trying to collect together ingredients for a parkin. They didn't have most of them but she didn't care, flinging all sorts of stuff into the pig trough. Then she threw off her old muddy shoes, jumped up into the trough and began to knead the dough with her grimy feet.

Billy looked on with his mouth open, and even Tom Puss up on the chimney stared down the flue with his fur all on end. They had seen Hepzibah in a rage before but never such a strange one. She jumped and thumped and paddled and stamped, shouting rude things about Mrs Greenaway all the while, until the dough was well mixed. Then she leapt from the trough and, dragging a huge baking sheet to the fire, she tipped the whole mess of dough out on to it, where it flopped into a sort of round cake as big as a cartwheel.

'Parkins is allus square,' Billy muttered, but he took care not to be heard.

Almost immediately something began to happen, something strange. The lump of dough began to rise just as if it had been properly made. It also began to cook at an amazing rate. In five minutes it was completely done and there it lay, big, round and brown, smelling rich and strange.

Hepzibah hauled it off the fire, not a single burn on it, and rolled the enormous thing across the room and pushed it out of the door.

'I'll show Mrs Greenaway how to make parkin, the old hag!' screamed Hepzibah, the light of madness in her eyes. 'And then I'll take the broomstick to you, my lad!'

As she crossed the threshold she tripped on one of her discarded shoes and lost her grip on the parkin. It began to roll down the hill.

'No!' shrieked Hepzibah, 'Come back here!' She picked herself up and ran after it. Her cries brought all the villagers out of their houses to see what was happening. There was the parkin bowling along down towards the ravine with Hepzibah staggering behind. At the edge of the ravine the parkin's mad career was halted for a moment as it hit a bush, but Hepzibah ran straight on clear over the edge and right into the hopeful dragon's mouth. GULP!

'THAT WASN'T VERY TASTY!' remarked the dragon with a cough, but just then the parkin dislodged itself from the bush and rolled into the gully right at the dragon's feet. 'COR!' he said and chomped at it with his big white teeth. Unfortunately they immediately became so stuck fast in it that he couldn't open his mouth.

Now when the villagers saw that, they thought it was a golden opportunity to get rid of the dragon once and for all. They all ran home and got their knives and axes and scythes and pitchforks and anything else they could lay their hands on. Then they ran back and tried to get down into the dragon's ravine. It was full of the fire that spurted through the dragon's teeth as he wrestled with the parkin. Even the rocks were too hot to climb on. But just then the dragon saved them the trouble by deciding to wash the parkin off in the sea. Spreading his wings he suddenly launched himself out of the ravine and kep-plopped himself down into the water. The villagers ran after him and, as soon as his head was underwater, they hit him again and again until he breathed in water and drowned.

When the victorious villagers marched back from the shore singing and rejoicing, they found the door to Billy's house open, everything clean and bright; a fine fire was burning on the hearth with a nice square parkin baking in front of it. Old Tom Puss was washing himself in the chimney corner and sitting at a scrubbed table with good food in front of him, was Billy. Mrs Greenaway was sitting placidly knitting in old Mrs Biter's chair by the fire. She nodded at them, but said nothing. From that day on she looked after Billy herself.

Out in the sea the dragon's body slowly hardened into stone. Folk nowadays call it Filey Brig.

The Witch Hare

Eskdale

Bad times throw up witches as rotten meat breeds flies. They are everywhere, friends, not kindly nature worshippers but malevolent haters of everything good. Harvests, animals, children, all are vulnerable to the witches' spite and demonic power. Who are the witches? It is often hard to be certain, but keep an eye on the outsiders, the ones who do not conform, the strange, the deformed, the sharp-tongued. Who else would wish us such harm? Who else would try to destroy so wantonly the wonderful world God has created for us? Watch your neighbours carefully, friends, and you will see the signs, catch the evil glance that brings murrain down on your cattle, hear the muttered spell as you pass.

Above all watch for the familiar spirits who appear in the form of animals: Mother Jenkins has a cat cleverer than any right cat should be; old Toby talks to crows; the hunchback who lives near the wood has a pet toad.

But that is not the worst of it, for witches themselves can turn into animals.

There was once a new plantation in Eskdale that was being destroyed by hares, a great quantity of hares, who nibbled off the tops of the little trees. The owner organised shooting parties to get rid of them, but there was always one that got away and it seemed to the hunters that each time it was the same hare.

The owner laid snares and sat up night after night trying to catch that last one, but without success. She set off the snares unharmed and even dodged bullets. It was clear to him that she must be a witch.

He discussed it with his friends and they all came to the conclusion that they should consult the Wise Man (a holy person, untainted by witchcraft, most thought him, though others felt that he pried too much into God's secrets).

They took him a present of honey and begged him to help them with a witch hare. He stroked his long white beard. 'The matter is easy,' he said. 'Give me a silver coin.'

He broke the coin into pieces. 'Load these pieces into your gun and shoot the hare with them. Silver bullets are a sovereign remedy for witches of all sorts.'

The following evening was warm and pleasant as the owner and his friends set off for the plantation with the gun. As they clattered down the main street of the village they passed a tiny cottage at the very end where an ugly old woman sat in her doorway, enjoying the late sun and carding wool. She greeted them and they muttered a reply, not daring to look at her directly, for everyone knows that old women can put the evil eye on you.

'How goes your plantation?' she asked the owner.

'Well enough,' he replied, walking briskly away. She spat on his shadow as it passed.

'Courtesy costs nowt!' she shouted after him.

The men reached the plantation and hid in the bushes to await the hare's appearance. The moon slowly rose and filled the valley with light. It grew cold, but the men sat patiently, still and silent. It was past midnight when they saw a movement among the little trees. A big grey hare was there, stretching up to nibble the juicy top of one of them.

The owner took careful aim with his silver-loaded gun and fired. The hare leapt and fell dead. The men waited cautiously to see if anything else would happen, but the hare didn't move. They cheered and slapped each other on the back. Then one of them ran to pick up the body.

'No! leave it!' shouted the owner. 'Who fancies eating a witch hare?' And so the body was left in the moonlight and the men all went home.

At dawn the next morning a milkmaid going to work was passing the tiny cottage at the end of town when she noticed that the door was open. She looked closer and found the old woman lying there dead in the doorway. Blood had dried around the wound at her heart, but of a bullet there was no sign.

The Drain Frog

Holderness
If you were to chop up several well-known fairy tales in a blender you might end up with the following tale, told by a Holderness woman in the late nineteenth century. The collector adds that he had often heard the same story from his nurse. It is a particularly odd local version of the Frog Prince.

There was once a frog who lived in the drain beneath a pump in a Holderness farm wash house. It was a spacious abode and he would have been happy enough but for one thing: whenever the women of the farm emptied dirty water – from washing mucky potatoes, or nappies, for example, or from making blood puddings – his sitting room became filled with unspeakable muck.

Now, the farmer's wife had died and he had remarried. His new wife already had a daughter the same age as his own, so he had fondly imagined that the two girls would become friends, but, as so often happens in stories, the stepmother thought her own daughter far superior to her stepdaughter and behaved accordingly. Poor Molly had to rise before dawn to light the fires and do the milking, whereas Clarice lay in bed until noon.

One day when she had been cleaning the grate, Molly poured a pailful of mucky water down the drain and began to pump a fresh one. Suddenly up the plughole came a small frog shaking its fist.

'It's too much! It really is! Tuesday's swede water was bad enough, but wet ashes are the last straw!'

The girl was very surprised but she'd been properly brought up.

'I'm very sorry, Sir, but please could you explain what's the matter?'

'Every time you empty dirty water down the drain it ruins my sitting room!'

Molly was very apologetic, explaining that she had no intention of upsetting him.

'In future,' she said, 'I shall empty my pail behind the house.'

The frog was touched. 'You're a kind girl! And as you've been so reasonable I shall give you a gift. From now on whenever you speak a pearl or a jewel will drop from your kind mouth.'

Well, it didn't take long for the stepmother to find out about the gift: a big pearl fell – splash! – into Molly's soup that very evening when she asked for the salt. Molly didn't want to tell her stepmother about the frog for fear that she would do something nasty to it, but the wretched woman nagged and pried and bullied until at last the girl told her the whole story.

'We'll see about that!' said the stepmother. 'I don't see why you should have something that poor Clarice does without.' She summoned her daughter (who was sitting on a fat cushion in the parlour, eating strawberries and clotted cream) and told her what to do.

'But Ma, I don't want to walk about with a nasty pail of dirty water!'

'Don't be silly! Don't you want to spout diamonds and pearls? In any case you don't have to do the work first. Just take one of the mucky pails off of Molly.'

The lazy daughter yawned, but the next time Molly walked past lugging a big bucket of soapy water Clarice took it off her and dragged it to the wash house (spilling half of it on her own shoes). She tipped it up and began pouring it down the drain. Oh how angry the frog was! It shot up the plughole shaking its little fist and shouting.

'You wicked girl! I thought we had an agree– Oh! You're a different one!'

He calmed down a bit then and explained the problem of the sitting room. Now even though the lazy daughter had been carefully told by her mother what she was supposed to say, when push came to shove she just couldn't bear being told off – especially by a frog.

'Just who do you think you are, Slimy!' she shouted angrily. 'This is my mother's house and you're only a nasty, dirty little squatter. If you're not careful I'll pour bleach down the drain. That'll clean you up! Now what about my gift?'

For a moment the frog was too surprised to speak. Then it said, 'Very well. I'll give you a gift for your words. You'll see,' and it dived down the drain out of her reach.

When the lazy daughter next met her mother she began to complain about the frog's rudeness, but she hadn't got very far before a slug and several small snakes fell out of her mouth. The mother and the daughter both screamed, but it was no use: lazy Clarice had to learn to speak seldom and carry a very large handkerchief.

Somehow the stepmother got it into her head that it was all Molly's fault. She behaved worse and worse to her, cuffing and slapping her, depriving her of food. She probably would have done her some real damage if it hadn't been for fear of her husband finding out. Molly didn't bother complaining to her father; it would have just been her word against that of her stepmother and sister. Instead she tried to keep out of the way.

One afternoon, Molly was sitting out in the yard (where she was now banished during mealtimes), eating a small piece of bread and cheese, when she heard a little voice singing:

Come bring me my food
My own, my sweet one!
Come bring me my food, my honey!

It was the frog, hopping across the yard towards her. 'Can you spare a tiny bit for me?' it asked, looking up at her with its lively black eyes.

'Of course!' she replied (automatically catching in her apron the ruby and pearl that fell from her mouth). She offered it a bit of her bread and cheese and they sat there in the sun nibbling companionably and chatting. It wasn't long, however, before the stepmother looked out of the window and saw Molly doing nothing.

'Get on with boiling that pig swill, you lazy slut!' she shouted.

As Molly regretfully left for the barn she looked back to
wave at the frog. It was staring after her with an affectionate
look on its green face.

'How nice to have a friend!' she thought. 'Even if it's only
a frog.'

That very night as she (last to bed as usual) was locking the
front door, she heard a little voice singing:

Take me to bed
My own, my sweet one,
Take me to bed, my honey!

She opened the door again and there was the frog sitting on the doorstep.

'Poor thing is lonely,' she thought. 'It's harmless enough.' She looked around but her stepmother was already safely tucked up in bed so she picked up the frog and popped it into her apron pocket. Then she locked the door and went upstairs to her draughty attic. She put the frog on top of her folded shawl at the end of her little truckle bed. Then she undressed, put on her nightdress and got in.

'Night, frog!'

'Night, Molly!'

She was soon asleep, but in the morning she found that the frog seemed to have become a lot heavier in the night, because she couldn't stretch her legs out. When she opened her eyes, there, sitting at the end of the bed, stark naked but modestly wrapped in her shawl and watching her with lively black eyes, was – yes, you've guessed it – a handsome prince!

Explanations, spell broken, stepmother forgiven, tears all round, wedding, happy ending!

The Hare and the Prickly Backed Urchin

Scarborough

It was a lovely morning in summer on Ganton Wold near Scarborough; just the sort of morning to please everyone, with skylarks singing and bees buzzing. The prickly backed urchin (hedgehog) was standing by his door, snuffing the breeze and humming to himself as folks do when they look out on a fine

Sunday morning. The idea came into his head that while his wife was doing the washing up he might as well have a stroll out, to see how his turnips were doing. The turnips were in a field next to his house and he and his family used to have a nibble at them from time to time (that was why he called them 'his').

He'd just got as far as the bullace bush at the corner of the field when he met the old hare. Hare was strolling too, looking at his cabbages. The urchin greeted the hare politely with 'Hoo's tha doin'?' but, instead of replying 'Middlin' thankee, hoo's thysen?', Hare snapped, 'What's thoo doin' out here all by thysen?'

'Just havin' a stroll around,' replied the prickly backed urchin.

'Havin' a stroll around?' laughed the hare. 'I'd a thought thoo could find something better for thy awd [old] bandy legs to do than to come spyin' on my cabbages!'

Now this nettled the prickly backed urchin. He could put up with a lot, but not insults to his legs – he was touchy on the subject.

'Thoo talks as if thoo'd got a better set thysen!'

'I should hope so,' said the hare smugly, casting an admiring glance down at his elegant long back legs.

'Well, I reckon I could show you the colour of my tail in a race.'

'Thoo's daft! Thoo and thy bandy legs. But I don't mind showing thee a thing or two. What's the stakes?'

'I'll lay a guinea and a bottle of gin!'

'Done!' said the old hare. 'Come on then, let's have it out NOW!'

'What's your hurry? I'm not ready yet. I hate to be rushed, tha knows. I have one or two things to do first. I'll meet you in half an hour.'

Well, the hare agreed to this and the urchin cantered off back home thinking, 'He thinks his long legs are so special, but I'll show him a thing or two afore I'm finished!'

When he got home he said to his wife, 'Look sharp Missus! Get thysen ready and come out with me.'

'Why? Whatever's up? Thoo hasn't bin out for a walk with me since I don't know when.'

'Never mind that. I've bet a guinea and a bottle of gin with the hare and I want thee with me.'

'Thoo's goin' to race the hare? Has thoo lost thy wits? Thoo knows he can run ten times faster nor thoo!'

'Now Missus,' he says, firm like, 'this is my job. Just get ready and come out with me.' So what could the prickly backed urchin wife do but go with him?

As they were going up to the place where the prickly backed urchin had arranged to meet the hare, he said to his wife (who was still objecting), 'Now shut up a minute. Whatever you say, I'm goin' to do this race in the turnip field. I shall run in one furrow and the hare in the next one. What thoo's got to do is to parzle [wander] off to the top end of the furrow near the bullace bush and sit there. We'll start from this end and when the old hare comes to the other end of the field all thoo has to do is to jump up and say "Here I am!"'

So the prickly backed urchin wife went up the furrow to the bullace bush and after he had given her time to get there the old urchin went to meet the hare. There he was, waiting to win his guinea and his bottle of gin. When he saw the urchin he said 'Is ta fit?' [Are you ready?]

'Aye, lad,' answered the urchin.

'Then come on!'

Each of them took his place at his furrow. The old hare counted 'One, two, three and away!' and off he went as fast as ever he could. The old urchin only ran a few yards; then he came back and lay down among the turnips at the start of the furrow.

The hare went loping up the field as fast as a steam engine, but when he got to the top out jumps the prickly backed urchin wife and calls out 'Here I am!'

It was rather a shock for the hare who had thought the urchin must be at least a hundred yards behind, but he didn't suspect anything because the prickly backed urchin wife looked for all the world like the prickly backed urchin. He thought to himself, 'This is a queer old job,' but he said

'Come on back then!' and off he went back down the furrow as fast as a steam engine. The prickly backed urchin wife stayed where she was.

When the old hare got to the other end of the field – Oh no! – out jumped the urchin and yelled 'Here I am!'

The hare was beside himself with rage. 'Once more!'

'All right, as often as you like!' retorted the urchin. And off the hare went once more.

This happened ninety-nine times and the prickly backed urchin won every time. By the hundredth lap the hare had had it. About halfway down the furrow he had a stroke, fell down and died. So the urchin took his guinea and his bottle of gin, called for his wife and off they went home, quite content with the morning's work. And if they haven't died since, they're still there.

The moral of this story is that you shouldn't be rude to your neighbours, no matter how superior you think you are.

2

THE SEA

SEA FOLK

Skinningrove

We used to watch you from the waves, you, the dry people, the land crabs. We thought you interesting in those days, seeing signs of intelligence, so we would sometimes follow the winged ships, watch your clever ways with ropes, capturing the wind to make it do the will of the stiff men who stood on the deck wrapped in tight blue skins. We thought of you as honorary sea people, breathing air like dolphins or whales. We often tried to help in those days, warning you of storms, though you never showed us any gratitude. Now-a-days, though, it is all different: we hate and fear you in your great noisy vessels, scooping up all the fish in the sea and leaving nothing behind but brightly coloured balls of strange dead stuff spawned into our water.

We sea people are long lived. Some of us still remember the days before we started to hate you, the days when we regarded you as amusing oddities. Here is a story from those times about an uncle of mine who was captured and forced to live on shore.

It was near one of your villages, Skinningrove, just up the coast from the village that fell into the sea (Runswick), that he was caught in a net and drawn out of our mother ocean by some local fishermen. Now, we had no quarrel with fishermen in those days; they hunted fish, just as we did, and they were careful to honour the sea and not to offend its peoples. These men could hardly believe their eyes when they saw my uncle with his smooth green skin and his fine dorsal fin and webbed fingers. They could not understand what he said for he had not learnt air speech and squeaked like a dolphin, but they carried him off and locked him into a sort of cave.

My uncle told me that he was afraid at first, but he realised after a while that they were not going to eat him, especially when one of them brought him a big basket of nice fish for his supper. He had always been a traveller, happy to explore waters where strange creatures lurked, and so he decided to use the opportunity to study his captors.

They seemed to fear him longer than he feared them. At first they peered over the top of the door at him, but after a while, thanks to his ability to put strangers at ease, some of them began to enter and even, strange though it may seem, to reciprocate his interest. They never got over his preference for raw fish and kept offering him other things, unable to believe that he wouldn't enjoy these treats as much as they did. My uncle occasionally tried the stuff, just to keep them happy, but he could never get any of it down. He said it was like eating mussel shells or a dead sponge.

One land crab in particular took a liking to my uncle. He was patterned like a killer whale, my uncle said, all black and white with a band of white around his neck. He came many times, and although my uncle and he couldn't understand each other's speech, they began to converse after a fashion using signs, as though they were both deaf.

The killer whale man showed my uncle that his black and white skin was just a set of coverings and could come off. He even tried to get my uncle to put a part of it on, seeming

worried that he had no covering of his own. Out of politeness my uncle tried to put this thing on, but his skin, already sore and itchy because he had been out of water so long, became inflamed. He also confided to me that although the killer whale man's skin smelt very unpleasant, he seemed to find my uncle's smell just as nasty, and sometimes backed away holding his nose.

It wasn't just men who came to see my uncle. Several young females who lived in the village often came in a bunch, giggling, to look into the door of his cave. He said they were quite pretty, though not as beautiful as mermaids, and that it gave him great pleasure to look at them. He said that they knew perfectly well how to attract a male and teased him delightfully when their menfolk were not around.

After being a captive for four moons, my uncle had been so long out of water that he was becoming weak and listless. The land folk saw this and began to argue with one another. In the end it was the killer whale man who insisted on my uncle's being let out of the cave for exercise. He was not allowed into the sea, though, and there were always people around to keep an eye on him.

Seeing that further study of land crabs would permanently damage his health, he was determined to escape and so pretended to be weaker than he really was. His watchers had no idea of how quickly he could move when he had to. One day he was playing ball with some of the young men when he simply galloped for the sea. Before they realised what had happened he was well out into the bay. At first they thought he would come back. Then, when they realised that he wasn't going to they waved and called to him. He said he felt a little sorry to be saying goodbye to all those who had been kind to him, specially the killer whale man, so he waved back quite a few times to show that there were no hard feelings. However, the feel of the sea on his skin, though it smarted at first, was so delightful that he soon started swimming and didn't stop until he was near Greenland.

He is very old now and his far-swimming days are over, but he will still talk to the young fry about his time on shore. Knowing what they do about trawlers and sonar, they think he must be telling fairy tales.

THE STAITHES MERMAIDS

Staithes

I and my sisters loved to hear my uncle's tales of his captivity. We played at capturing each other when we were young and would fight over who got to be killer whale man. As we got older we sometimes – though it was strictly forbidden by our parents – swam close to shore in fine weather to sing to the fishermen and tease them by pretending we were in love with them.

Secretly we each dreamed of meeting a handsome young fisherlad but we never saw anyone you would call a mermaid's dream and had to make do with the teasing.

We played other games too. I remember my sister Charis would sometimes surface near a boat and stand on her tail, combing her golden hair to make the men on board think that a storm was in the offing. Sometimes there was, sometimes there wasn't, but it was always fun to watch them rushing about preparing to haul in the nets. We were always careful to avoid the actual places where the nets were set, though; we had no real desire to be captured.

One day, about two hundred years after our uncle's capture, we were swimming along the edge of the land with a pod of dolphins, hunting herring. It was the warm season when they were plentiful, swimming towards their spawning grounds further north. We were frisky, leaping out of the water with the dolphins, for we could all feel the fizzyness that means a change in the weather. We knew that a storm was brewing up.

My sister Charis and I were not afraid of storms – out in the ocean you can always swim into deep water and be safe – but on this occasion we were so carried away by excitement and the dolphins' exhilaration that we stayed too close to shore. When the storm broke we began to be dashed hither and thither by the waves that broke over the shallow beds of chalk near the shore. We are both strong swimmers, but this storm was more powerful than any we had known, and in those days we had little experience of onshore winds. Despite our efforts, the waves would carry us inshore towards the rocks and we would have to fight our way out again. It was fun at first, but as night came on and the dolphins departed, we began to get tired. It was Charis who first suggested that we haul ourselves out on shore and wait until morning when the storm would have blown itself out.

We found a little beach at one side of a huge rocky cliff and pulled ourselves up the beach in a torrent of rain. There were upturned boats there, pulled above the tide line for safety, so we knew that land folk must be close by, but we were so tired that we scrambled into hiding behind the boats and, despite the thunder and wind, fell as fast asleep there on the pebbly shore as if we were being rocked in the deep.

When we opened our eyes the following morning, it was to find ourselves in the same predicament as our uncle. The reality was not nearly as much fun as our games had been; we were surrounded by a ring of frowning faces, all men and boys, squawking away like puffins, their horrible little eyes popping out of their heads. They smelt very nasty.

I had learned some words of air speech over the years, but they spoke too fast for me to understand. I tried saying very slowly and loudly 'We Friends! You help us!' but it didn't seem to do any good. Before we could escape they had thrown nets over us and started hauling us away. We shouted and threatened them with all the evil things we could think of, but to no avail. They dragged us roughly up to their little village and shut us in what my uncle would have called a cave, but we, being better educated, knew was a stable. It was dark and dirty and smelt of some sort of land creature, whose dung was all over it. Then they pulled off the nets and began to handle us in a most indecent and offensive way. Some of the men touched our golden hair and even drew their filthy fingers through it. Others ran their hands over our beautiful tails. One or two even fondled our breasts as though they had never seen such things before – indeed, we never saw any of their females' breasts, so it is possible that, like fish, they don't have any.

All the time they talked very loudly and rudely to each other, never to us. They stole, and then squabbled over, my coral necklace and Charis' pearls.

In the end they made so much noise that their womenfolk came to see what was happening. They did not seem at all pleased at our capture. They shouted and screamed at the men. Then they threw lumps of dung at us. In the end everyone went out, locking the door behind them and leaving us in the dark, sore and bruised.

Either our uncle had lied or times had changed considerably, because no kind person came to try talking to us. Young boys came to stare at us and then threw mud over the top of the door or shouted what we guessed were rude things. The women who fed us brought only the oldest and most disgusting fish, slapping or pinching us if we didn't move quickly enough. It was not at all what we expected.

After some days an old land crab appeared. He had a black skin garment with a very white front and a white band around his neck just like a killer whale, as my uncle had said. At first we thought it must be the one uncle had met, but land crabs live such short lives that I suppose it can't have been. He was holding two sticks, bound one across the other, which he held up in front of himself as if for protection. Then he ranted at us, saying, as far as I could understand, that we were naked demons sent to drag all the young men to Hull. I said hello, that I was a friend, and that we wanted to go back to the sea, not Hull, but he shook his head, saying that we would just return to lure the young men away. All the time he was talking he was staring at our breasts, as though they were some delicious fish he wanted to catch.

Charis was cleverer than me. She wriggled up to him (it was hard to get along that knobbly floor) and looked beseechingly at him with her big brown eyes until he went as red as a mullet and fairly ran out of the stable. That got rid of him, but he remembered to lock the door.

I don't know whether the people of Staithes (that was the name of the village) were crueller than those of Skinningrove, where our uncle had been captured, or whether they just hated females more, but for the entire time we were held prisoners we did not meet with one kindness. Insults, blows, stones and mud we had in plenty, however, until we feared that they would eventually kill us.

Our escape was sudden and unexpected. The man whose stable it was – he lived not far away at a place called Jackdaw's Well – allowed us out once a week to haul ourselves around the filthy yard while he mucked out our prison. Sometimes he let visitors pay whatever the land crabs use for pearls to watch us. We were pretty filthy ourselves by this time, our hair lank, our skins beginning to break into sores, but the land crabs who paid didn't seem to be able to get enough of us and complained when we were locked up again.

On one particularly rainy day no one had come to watch us and so our gaoler was careless; he hadn't noticed that the outside gate had failed to shut properly. We bided our time and when he went into the stable to change our water bowls, we fled as fast as we could, slithering through the gate and humping ourselves over the cobble stones down the slipway towards the water.

The land crab ran after us, shouting, holding a pole with a sharp hook at the end. We gasped and gasped, tearing scales off our tails as we covered the last remaining stretch of ground and fell into our Mother Water. Though we were weak, two strokes of our tails took us easily out of his reach among the boats moored by the quay. Other land crabs, hearing shouts, came running down; some got into their boats to chase us; others threw the usual things; all shouted, but soon we were far out into the harbour. I would have kept going, but my sister wouldn't leave without calling down revenge on our tormentors. She had become pretty good at air speech by this time, though she never let on to the land crabs. She stood up on her tail and shouted over the water, 'People of Staithes! Hear my words. We were helpless guests on your shore, but you treated us worse than barnacles. The sea will drink at Jackdaw's Well before you will be forgiven!'

'Threaten away!' one man shouted back. 'Jackdaw's Well is a tidy way inland!'

The curse stuck, of course, Charis being a sea daughter; the wind blew and the sea rose, drowning many houses and people in Staithes, all the way to Jackdaw's Well, which was permanently turned salt, but by then we had swum together into deep water, vowing never, never to venture near land again.

ROBIN HOOD TURNS FISHERMAN

Robin Hood's Bay
Have you ever heard the tale of how Robin Hood grew sick of the greenwood and decided to take a holiday?

'But where will you go?' asked Little John.

'Scarborough!' replied his leader. 'I fancy the seaside.'

'Scarborough? But there's nought there but fishermen. No one to rob; no deer; just stinking fish! What will you find to do?

'I was thinking that I might turn fisherman myself – just for a little while. I could call myself Simon Wise …'

Robin stood on the quay in Scarborough looking at the bobbing boats and sniffing the fishy salt air. Seeing a fisherman mending nets not far from him, he asked whether there was anywhere he could rent a room for a while. The man looked him up and down.

'Thoo's not from around here,' he observed. 'What art thoo?'

'I'm a fisherman!'

The man stared at him and then began to laugh. 'If thoo's a fisherman then I'm Angel Gabriel!' He laughed so much that he began to choke and Robin had to bang him on the back. Finally he leant back gasping with tears in his eyes. 'Try Widow Waddilove,' he managed. 'Small house in front of the town cross.'

Widow Waddilove was pleased to have such a fine strapping lodger. Her husband had been a fisherman with his own boat but he had been lost in a storm, leaving her with four small children. They clustered hopefully around this strange tall man, their round eyes big in their hungry faces. When she heard that this kind Master Wise was prepared to pay her double what she had asked for a bed, the Widow, in tears, insisted on giving Robin her own room, while she and all the children squashed into the room at the back of the little house.

The next morning, sitting down to a fine breakfast provided by Robin, she asked him what he intended to do in Scarborough.

'I thought I might try to get a job on a boat,' said her new lodger.

The Widow blinked. 'Forgive me, Master Wise, but thoo doesn't look much like a fisherman.'

Robin frowned; he was getting a little annoyed at the repeated doubt. 'Why not? I'm strong and handy,' he retorted, 'what's wrong with me helping with the fishing?'

'I beg your pardon, master,' said the Widow, 'but does thoo know awt of the sea? She's a wicked chancy old thing even if one's lived by her for a lifetime, as my man found out. But anyway our Scarborough men'll never take a landsman who knows nowt of local traditions and beliefs. It'd be bad luck and luck is everything at sea.'

'We'll see about that!'

But Widow Waddilove was right. When Robin approached the fishing boats and explained that he wanted work, there wasn't a single man who would take him. Being, for the most part, kind men, they all had some apparently good excuse or other, but Robin returned to the Widow's house much disheartened; he wasn't used to rejection.

'Well, Master Wise,' she said, 'did I not warn thoo? But cheer up now, I've spoken to my cousin Ralph who's grateful for tha help of me and mine and he's agreed to give thoo a trial for a couple of days. No share of the fish, mind, while [until] thoo proves thyself able.'

The following morning before dawn she took him down to the harbour and introduced him to her cousin Ralph, a big man with a weather-beaten face even browner than Robin's, where it was not covered by a vast black beard. He looked Robin up and down.

'Well thoo looks strong enough, Master Wise. So, do what th'art told, keep clear of the ropes and we'll see what we can make of thoo. Come aboard the *Kathryn*.'

The three other men crewing the big coble [a flat-bottomed fishing boat] stared at Robin in an unfriendly way and muttered to each other, but Ralph was the skipper and what the skipper said, went.

As the day progressed it became clear that Robin was not much of an asset. The fish were caught on long lines of hooks, weighted with stones at one end and buoyed with cork at the other. Each man had charge of his own, coiled in the bottom of the boat. When they reached the fishing grounds, each paid out his lines over the side so that they lay across the incoming tide. It took skill. Robin didn't realise that they first had to be baited and there were derisive shouts when he tried to put the bare hooks over the side.

Other problems soon arose: he loosed the wrong rope and dropped the little lug sail on his own head; he didn't know what 'Going about' meant so that when the boat changed tack he was nearly knocked overboard by the beam; he didn't know halliards from stays or larboard from starboard. That was bad enough but he committed worse crimes because he didn't know any of the fishermen's superstitions: he whistled a careless tune, waved to a priest walking on the shore, and even mentioned PIGS! These were all known to be causes of such bad luck that it was only out of respect to Ralph that Master Wise was still alive by the end of the day.

'I say we throw Master Stupid overboard NOW!' snarled Brom Jenkinson, the surliest of the crew. 'He's nowt but a Jonah! We'll never catch no fish with him aboard and come home drownded into the bargain!' The others growled agreement.

Ralph looked worried. 'I hear what thoo says,' he said, 'but he's been right good to my cousin and he doesn't know our ways. Give him one more day and if he don't shape up I'll set him back on shore.'

'Waste of good fishing weather!' muttered the others, but they agreed to let Robin stay for another day.

That night Robin curled up wet and tired in the bottom of the boat, heartily wishing himself back in the greenwood. No one had offered him either food or drink and his big bowman's hands, tough enough from plucking the bowstring, were blistered by pulling ropes in salt water. 'I'll show 'em!' he muttered, falling into an exhausted sleep.

The next day he managed better, largely because no one let him do anything. The boat followed the coast most of the day, casting its lines every so often. By the afternoon they had hauled in a sizeable catch and the men seemed a little friendlier.

As they prepared to set sail for Scarborough, however, Robin, who had been doing little but staring at the view, said, 'Master Ralph, there's a sail moving up quickly from behind that headland. I know I'm no judge, but it doesn't look like a fishing boat.'

Ralph peered at it with narrowed eyes. The boat beneath the sail was long, swift and black. 'God's Bones lads!' he shouted. 'Run for home! Run for home! Get that sail up! It's the French!' Instantly the others jumped to the ropes and raised the sail. The *Kathryn* began to gather speed.

'It's all the fault of that Jonah!' growled Brom Jenkinson. 'I knew we should have thrown him overboard! Them French monkeys'll take our fish and drown us into the bargain!'

'We're not at war with them again, are we?' asked Robin. 'Or are they pirates?'

'Who knows?' replied Ralph. 'They may be cousins of the King of France for owt I can say, but, time out o' mind, they've been filthy false robbers of fishing boats up and down this coast. God damn this wind! We'll have to row for it lads.'

Robin watched the French boat shooting over the water, altering its course to intercept them. He might not be a sailor but he know an approaching disaster when he saw it. Swiftly he calculated the distance between the boats.

'I reckon I can take the steersman out easy,' he said, stretching and cracking his knuckles. The others, struggling to get the oars out, stared at him as if he'd gone mad. 'I can shoot him. With my bow,' he added. He rummaged around in the thwarts of the boat where he had stowed his things when he came on board.

'Fitted nicely along the side, see? It's a bit wet, but I've got the bowstring in my pocket.' Four mouths hung open as he bent the mighty six-foot longbow and strung it.

'Arrows too!' he pointed out triumphantly, pulling a sheaf from beneath his blanket. 'Never go anywhere without 'em,' he explained.

Ralph shook his head. 'Simon mate, thoo's brave but thoo's also cracked. Thoo'll never do it!'

'Listen,' said Robin, shaking his head. 'It's very simple. You're fishermen. I'm a bowman. You know your work and I know mine. I'll just set my back against the mast and you'll see what I mean.'

No one argued; the French boat with its better sails was gaining on them in leaps and bounds. Robin braced his back against the little mast and took careful aim.

'It's a tricky shot,' he commented calmly, 'but no worse than shooting at running deer from the back of a galloping horse. Now that's looking good –'

THWACK! The French helmsman started violently and fell back. The French boat veered wildly, its sail flapping as it came up into the wind. The crew of the *Kathryn* cheered and shouted with amazed glee.

Robin carefully chose another arrow and shot a tall Frenchman who seemed most likely to be the captain. As he too fell, Robin sent arrow after arrow flying over the water into the French boat. Each one found its mark and soon no more heads could be seen looking over the side. The boat swung and rolled in the water, unmanned.

Robin was pleased with his own shooting but not as pleased as the crew of the *Kathryn*. They thumped him on the back and called him every good name they could think of, apologising for their previous rudeness.

'There's no time for this,' he told them. 'Aren't we going to board her?'

The French boat was three times the size of the *Kathryn*, but when Robin and the rest climbed aboard (knives held between their teeth like pirates themselves) the only enemies they met were dead men, each with one of Robin's peacock-feathered arrows in his chest.

Ralph had stayed at the *Kathryn*'s tiller, watching anxiously and listening for any sound of fighting. He could see nothing because the sides of the French boat was so much higher than his own. Suddenly there was a great shout. Were there men hidden in the hold? No, surely that was the sound of a heavy object being dragged. He waited, his heart thumping anxiously, his knife ready in his hand; slowly an object appeared above the side of the French boat; something large and black.

'Hey Master Ralph!' shouted Robin, his face appearing cheerily above the massive leather chest. 'We've caught some goldfish that should keep you happy!'

Heaving and swearing, they managed to get the chest into the *Kathryn* and then Ralph saw what Robin had been talking about: the chest was full of French gold; at least a thousand pounds!

'And so,' said Little John when his leader had finished telling his tale and was leaning back against a great oak in the greenwood, a mug of beer in one hand and a slice of venison pasty in the other. 'What's happened to all this gold? I don't see any sign of it!' Robin looked a little shifty. 'You've given it all away again, haven't you?'

'Well, I had to give half to the Widow,' said Robin. 'She and the children needed it.'

'And what about the rest? Surely you didn't give any to those evil fishermen? They nearly threw you overboard!'

'The fact is,' said Robin gaily, 'I was so pleased to get back to dry land that I gave them the other half. Don't look at me like that. I brought you all back some kippers, didn't I? Anyway, what's next? Now I'm up for some good old-fashioned robbing of the rich … Hark! Isn't that the sound of horses on the road …?'

BEGGAR'S BRIDGE

Eskdale
The River Esk flows sprightly and fast from its source high in Westerdale into the North Sea at Whitby, bringing stories with it. At Glaisdale it flows beneath the Beggar's Bridge, built to commemorate an enduring love.

Fair days at Egton, a village on the Esk, are still something special, but in the past they lasted for eight exciting days, attracting people from all over the area. There was a boy called Tom, soon to be apprenticed to a shipowner in Hull, who was staying with relatives in Egton during one such fair. He and his mate, Jack, were not rich, but they went to the fair intent on having a good time.

Among other fair-goers were Squire Richardson of Glaisdale, his daughter Agnes and her maid. The squire was a well-to-do man, keen on buying some good cattle. His daughter and the maid, Jane, however, had no such interest and, when he showed every intention of spending the precious visit talking cows with like-minded friends, they begged to be allowed to see more of the fair. The squire hummed and hawed – who knew what two such young girls might get up to? – but just then he caught sight of a particularly fine brindled heifer being led past. 'Very well, just for an hour or so,' he said, his eyes still on the heifer's tail, 'but don't talk to any young men.'

This was Elizabethan England, when jokes were broad and girls rather less dainty than they were to become later. In half an hour Agnes and Jane were being shown all the fun of the fair by two jolly young lads and enjoying themselves far more than their usually quiet life allowed. The girls had been targeted instantly by Tom and Jack, even though the boys could see by their clothes that they were far above them in status. All four sparred verbally as young people do, but Tom and Agnes were instantly attracted. They peeked surreptitiously at one other as they all went together through the fair.

There was a lot to see. They marvelled at the two-headed goat, laughed at the puppet show and shrieked when the Devil appeared to accompanying fireworks. The girls wept over the poor bear being baited and refused to let the boys enter a wrestling match. At one tempting stall Tom offered to buy Agnes a gilded gingerbread baby (causing general hilarity), which she blushingly refused.

'Well, then, I'll buy it for Jane and she shall give it to you so that your conscience may be clear.' But Jane too refused the offer; she knew better than to annoy Squire Richardson. Unwillingly she remembered that she was supposed to be keeping an eye on her lady.

'Listen, Mistress Agnes, the clock is chiming. The hour your father gave us is well and truly past. We should return to him.' She looked anxiously into Agnes' face as she spoke, but Agnes was looking at Tom and Tom at Agnes. It was plain as a pikestaff what was happening.

'You go back to the Buck Inn, Jane,' said Agnes. 'I will follow in a minute. Go!' she added fiercely as Jane tried to object.

Fortunately for Jane, Squire Richardson was still deep in bovine talk when she arrived at the inn. Jack, who had accompanied her, snatched a clumsy kiss and left her there. 'Don't you worry, lass. Tom'll see her safe back,' were his parting words, and indeed Agnes was back not long after, her big brown eyes shining, a little smile on her lips.

It took a while, but eventually Jane teased the cause of that smile out of her. She said that she was now betrothed to Tom. Jane was horrified, but not as horrified as Squire Richardson when Tom presented himself at the inn at the end of the day and asked for his daughter's hand. In those days, if two people promised to marry each other, even if they did it in secret, it was a serious thing, a promise made before God, and binding in a court of law. The squire was not a cruel man, so he did not try, as another might have done, to beat his daughter into repudiating her betrothal. However, he was absolutely adamant that if Agnes married Tom she would do so without his blessing. Respect for one's parents was very strong then, so, reluctantly, Agnes promised her father that she would not marry Tom unless he agreed – and anyway, without the father's blessing there would be no money for the young couple to live on.

The squire knew better than to forbid Tom to come to the house altogether. Inquiries soon told him that Tom was no vagrant but had a respectable, though poor, moorland sheep farmer as his father. He relied on time to wear out this sudden attachment. 'They'll grow tired of waiting and we'll hear no more of secret engagements!' he thought to himself. 'Besides, our house is on t'other side of the Esk from Egton. Wading that river'll cool his ardour!'

In those days there was no bridge over the Esk. There were fords, of course, but they were far apart and between them the river was difficult, and sometimes dangerous, to cross. Tom, however, was young and determined. Having settled on the girl he wished to marry, he was not going to give up. Once his apprenticeship started he had little free time, but whenever he could he walked up to Glaisdale and bravely crossed the river to Agnes' house. In dry weather the crossing was not too bad – there were slippery stepping stones of a sort – but if it rained he had to wade precariously, and when the river was in flood there was nothing else for it but to walk the long miles back to Egton.

Seeing Tom arrive so often wet and bedraggled, the squire expected that his daughter would soon be put off, but no! Tom's persistence made him a real hero for her and she loved him all the more. It was impossible for them to meet alone; Agnes' father and mother always made sure that a servant was present. However, the two managed to devise a way of meeting secretly. Agnes' bedroom was on the first floor, looking out over the Esk Valley towards Egton. She would put a candle on the windowsill whenever her parents were due to be away from home. When Tom saw the light shining out in the night he knew that next day he would be able to steal a few hours alone with Agnes, walking in Arncliffe Wood.

Because he was now a sailor, Tom was often away for weeks or even years at a time. His boyish good looks weathered and his shoulders broadened. His hands grew calloused and harsh from handling ropes, but still he returned to see his love, bringing with him tales of his adventures. In 1587 he sailed to the West Indies with the English fleet under his hero, Sir Francis Drake. There he saw many strange sights that had the whole Richardson household hanging on his words. He also brought back curious gifts for the family, grudgingly received by the squire, but delighting Agnes.

It was not long after this that the squire's patience finally wore out. His daughter had to be married while there were still suitors willing to offer for her, but time was running out, and, if she persisted in waiting for a man who was not only poor, but likely to be killed or drowned in some sea battle, she would soon be left on the shelf – and on the squire's hands. Something had to be done.

Catching Tom once more in the house one day, he finally forbade him to visit again.

'I have waited long enough for this foolishness to end. I shall never give my consent for my daughter to marry a beggarly sailor. You are wasting her time and mine as well. This must be the end of the matter. Agnes' future happiness depends on it.'

'And what if I should make my fortune, Sir? There are many opportunities at sea that a landsman will never encounter.'

The squire snorted in derision. 'Aye, well then: you make your fortune and you can have her, but be quick about it for she'll not wait much longer.'

Tom looked the old squire full in the face. 'I think she will, Sir. Thank you.'

In 1588, when Tom was twenty, the country was in turmoil. There was talk of a Spanish invasion. It seemed that Philip II of Spain, who had been married to the queen's half-sister Mary, had decided to come and claim the kingdom, returning it to Catholicism once again. It was rumoured that a hundred and thirty great ships were coming in May, bringing thousands of soldiers. Soon bonfire chains spread the terrible news that the Spanish fleet, the Armada, had sailed. All sailors of the English fleet were summoned back to their ships to defend the country under Sir Francis Drake. Tom had to go and he knew that his chances of returning were slim: sailors' lives were always dangerous, but sea battles were notorious for their casualties. It was very likely that he would never see Agnes again. He might have been officially banned from the house but he was not going to war without saying goodbye and he knew that the family servants were fond enough of him to find a way of letting the couple meet one last time.

That spring had been a rainy one. The ground was sodden underfoot and long before he reached the bank of the Esk, Tom could hear it roaring in flood. Yellow and foam-filled it poured down from the moors, carrying with it branches and debris from further up the valley. The noise beat on his ears and soon his clothes were wet with spray as he walked up and down the bank, looking for some place to cross. It was no use. The river was not particularly deep, but the force of the rushing water would have knocked him off his feet immediately, to be crushed against the rocks.

At last he stood still, staring up at the moor across the river, where Agnes' house shone in the early morning sun, barely a mile off, but unreachable. He picked up a rock and hurled it savagely into the river. 'If I'm spared,' he shouted into the din, 'I'll build a bridge across you, so help me God!'

The following morning, having walked to Whitby, Tom boarded his ship and set sail south, heading towards war and the great Armada.

Over the next few months his faith in his hero, Drake, was fully justified. God may have obligingly blown with His winds to disperse the enemy, as it says on the Armada portrait of Queen Elizabeth, but He got plenty of help from Drake,

Hawkins, Frobisher and Howard. The Spanish ships were driven away from the South Coast; England was safe, and even a lowly seaman like Tom could feel that he had had a part in her saving. His bravery was noticed and commended by Drake who asked him to join in other, rather more lucrative, expeditions. There were plenty of rich Spanish ships bringing gold and silver from the New World and for an ambitious young man the word 'piracy' held no fears. Tom rose quickly in his profession; he was only twenty-four when he sailed triumphantly into London docks with a captured Spanish ship.

Now, almost overnight, his fortune had been made. The ship and its contents sold for a very good price, enough to set Tom up as a gentleman. It was a very different Tom Ferris who returned in some style to claim the hand of Agnes Richardson. His years with Drake had taught him many things, educated him in the arts as well as the ways of the world. Squire Richardson (who didn't at first recognise him), looked at his gold laced suit, gulped and acted as if he'd always known Tom would make good. What Agnes thought of this changed Tom she kept to herself, but she had steadfastly refused all other suitors and she was happy enough to marry him and move to a fine house in Hull where Tom set himself up in business, running a shipping company.

They had twenty-two happy years together, during which Tom prospered, became the Sheriff of Hull and eventually mayor. Then, in 1618, Agnes died and Tom, looking back on their life together, remembered, now that he was lonely and grieving, the vow he had made on the night they were parted by the flood. A colder stream parted them now, but it eased his heart a little to keep his promise; he built a bridge across the River Esk as a tribute to Agnes.

In 1619 the bridge, which is now known as Beggar's Bridge, was completed and despite the floods that have swept later bridges away, it still stands as a lasting memorial to their faithfulness.

THE PRESS GANG

Scarborough
Let other places fear giants, ghosts, devil dogs and dragons. Up and down the coastal towns of England they feared something much more human: the press gang.

By long tradition the Royal Navy filled up any gaps in its manpower by legally kidnapping men in seaside towns and giving them the choice of 'volunteering' to join the Navy – in which case they were paid – or working unwillingly for it unpaid.

Those caught would be whisked away from their family, without even a farewell, to face an uncertain fate, possibly for years. There were a few reserved occupations but in time of war the press gang were none too choosy and, unless you actually had papers on you proving that you belonged to one of these occupations, or had wealthy friends prepared to pay the gang off, then you were done for.

The resentment and hatred this practice created, especially in the North, where men didn't take kindly to official interference with their lives, often broke out into pitched battles between townsfolk and the press gang. The Mayor of York was once threatened with being burnt in his own Mansion House when he had members of the press gang staying with him.

Fear of impressment haunts folk song and story; the public outrage felt about anyone who helped the press gang is reflected in the following story.

In one of the gullies that run up from the sea between Whitby and Robin Hood's Bay lived Farmer Mossburn and his two daughters, Hester and Dorothy. Being handsome lasses they had many admirers, but the lads they had given their hearts to were two brothers, Bill and Peter, two fisherlads who were off with the fishing fleet in Greenland waters. The young people had met at dances and markets, and fallen for one another immediately. The lads, however, were too shy to do anything serious about their affection before they went away. They knew that Farmer Mossburn would never wed his girls to lads without a good bit of brass behind them, so they meant to wait until the trip was over.

Fishing was one of the few ways in which a poor lad could make himself a fortune honestly. A plough boy would never rise much above farm manager, but a lucky fisherman could, in one season, bring back enough fish to set him up for a good long time.

The lads may also have been not quite sure about the Mossburn girls suitability as fishermen's wives, no matter how much they liked them. After all, they were farmer's daughters not from a fishing family. Choosing a good wife was a tricky business for a fisherman: she had to be faithful – all those trips away put a strain on any marriage – and resourceful – she would have to keep the household going, the children fed and the wolf from the door no matter how long her fisherman husband was away.

However, as the months of the trip wore away, Bill and Peter grew more and more decided about their choices. In the freezing sleet, their hands red raw pulling in nets, waves breaking over the boat, they kept themselves warm with the thought of the Mossburn girls.

'But what about Polly,' teased Peter. 'I thought tha was sweet on her. She'll likely hezzle tha hide for thee!'

'Give ower Peter. I've niver thought of her. She were just the entertainment of a moment.'

'Ah, but what does she think about thee?'

The trip turned out to be very successful and the shipowner was so pleased with Peter and Bill that he promised to give them their own boat to command the following year. As soon as they decently could after arriving at home, they smartened themselves up in finery bought with their first big pay and headed along the beach towards the Mossburn farm. As luck would have it – or perhaps she had planned it – they met the very Polly that Bill had once liked.

'Hello Bill,' she said, swinging her skirt. 'Tha's very dapper! I heard tha was returned. Does tha want a stroll wi' me? It's a weary while since I've seed thee.'

Bill went as red as a rose; he really hadn't given her a moment's thought except when Peter teased him. He had a good heart, though and didn't want to hurt her feelings.

'Nay, Polly. I'm sorry, but I canna gan wi' thee – I've got other fish to fry,' he added lamely. Polly stared at him. She was a tall, strongly built lass, rough-haired and freckled like most Whitby girls; well enough in her way, but not a patch on Hester, Bill thought.

'Is tha thinking on Hester Mossburn?' Polly's voice was scornful now. 'A farmer's daughter? She's not the one for thee!'

The brothers exchanged glances. 'I told you so!' Peter's glance implied. 'Wheesht, lass,' he said, 'Bill knows what he's about. He and Hester agree like church bells.'

'Oh aye!' sneered Polly. 'I know, they want naught but hanging. It's an old joke.'

'Well now, Polly. Mebbe we'll fix that matter tonight.'

Polly stared at them as she realised what he was saying. She had made plans concerning Bill while the brothers were away. Now she saw them disappointed. But she was no milk-and-water country maid; she was a tough fisherlass as ready with her fists as her tongue. Bill had the cheek to prefer another girl to her and so her heart was filled with rage, rather than grief. She drew herself up, blue eyes flashing, 'Curse Hester Mossburn! Curse the two of you!' and she fled away like the wind.

'Curses come home to roost, lass!' shouted Peter after her, but she had gone.

Bill looked stricken. 'Give her no mind,' said Peter, flinging an arm around his shoulders. 'Think on Hester!'

They continued on their way and soon began to climb up towards the farm. The farm dogs began to bark and before long the lads were standing nervously at the farm door.

'Mebbe they'll have forgotten us?' whispered Peter, but at that moment the door flew open and the two girls rushed out.

'We heard the dogs!' laughed Hester, flushing pink as Bill kissed her. 'We guessed it was you!' added Dorothy, equally pink. 'Ma told us the boat was back!'

What did they all do then? They walked and talked and kissed. It all went easy as an old shoe. Before Mrs Mossburn had laid the tea table the two couples were agreed. By the time the kettle had boiled they were standing before her, hand in hand, telling her their news. It was possibly not as much of a surprise as they expected because she had been peering out of the kitchen window, keeping an eye on them all for the last hour. She was, of course, delighted, though she couldn't resist, in her Yorkshire way, throwing a little darkness over their joy: 'Eh dear, but I don't know how your father will tek it ...'

The farmer dispelled her doubts; he had heard how profitable the fishing trip had been and he was delighted that his lasses would be so well settled with such hard-working lads. It was a very noisy tea; the young people, their eyes shining, joked and laughed and teased. Their parents joined in with a will, genuinely happy for them.

'So when shall we be wed?' asked Hester.

'A double wedding!' said her mother. 'After next year's trip? Say a year today?'

'A year!' scoffed the farmer, 'Can't you see how things are with them, Nellie? No! A wedding as soon as possible, I think. Why wait if they're agreed?'

And so they settled on a date for the following month and the rest of the evening was spent making plans. There was so much to do, as their mother kept exclaiming.

At last, as it was getting very late, the farmer tactfully reminded the lads that they should start home before the tide came in if they wanted to walk along the beach. Peter and Dorothy got up.

'And where does tha think tha's gannin', Dorothy Mossburn?' demanded her mother.

'I'll just say goodbye to Peter. I'll only be a few minutes!'

'Five minutes!' shouted her mother after her.

But the five minutes became fifteen. Mrs Mossburn shook her head and started muttering. Then all the dogs began to bark and a second later the door was flung open and Dorothy rushed in, her face pale, her eyes big with fear.

'The press gang!' she shouted. 'They've getten Peter! Dad! Bill! If you're men you'll save him! Quick!'

No need for more words! What fisherman cared a straw for the king's Navy? The press gang were more enemy than the French. Both men were up and out of the house in a moment. The terrified women heard shouts and the thump of punches. Then, except for the barking dogs, all went quiet.

'Have they killed them?' whispered Mrs Mossburn. 'Oh girls, what's happened to tha father? Oh George!'

'Be still, mother,' said Hester, putting her hand on her mother's shoulder. 'Dorothy and I will go out and see. You stay here – don't worry, we'll be alright!'

Gingerly, she and Dorothy opened the door and looked out. Their father lay motionless, not far from the gate. With a shriek the girls ran to him. He was still alive, though unconscious, but of Peter and Bill there was no sign: the press gang had taken them.

Farmer Mossburn recovered, though he retained no memory of the fight. Months went by and no news of the boys reached the family, though they did hear of the glorious victories won at sea by our gallant men against the demon Napoleon.

'Hearts of Oak are our ships,' people sang, 'jolly tars are our men!'

The Mossburn girls did not have hearts of oak. News of every battle filled them with fear for their own jolly tars. So many ships sunk! So many men dead! It seemed impossible that Bill and Peter could have survived. Unable to express their cruel anxiety in any other way, the two girls began to wear black.

The fish auction down on the staithe at Whitby was always a noisy, occasionally rambunctious, event. Everyone felt free to shout jokes or obscenities at each other or the auctioneer. Polly was there one day with the other fisherlasses, flyting, as they called it, with the men (coarser than flirting, less violent than fighting). One of Polly's comrades was telling all the girls how she had been jilted by her sweetheart and the others were commiserating with her.

'If a lad broke faith wi' me,' bragged Polly loudly, 'I'd soon get revenge. I'd show him how I can punish. You ask Hester Mossburn!'

Everyone heard her, even the men. A sudden silence fell. All eyes turned in her direction. An old fisherman, who was standing near Polly, grabbed her arm. He looked deep into her eyes. 'Is tha false, Polly?' he growled. 'Is tha? I would never have believed that such a stony heart lived among us.'

Muttering began to spread as the meaning of what he had said sank in. The old man gave her a violent push. The men against whom he pushed her thrust her away as though she had the plague.

She stood tall, intending to give them a sample of the language for which fisherlasses were famous, but there was something in the grim looks all around that stopped her. In that moment she knew that she had gone forever beyond the bounds of their pity. She fled, pursued by oaths and stinking fish heads.

As the news of her treachery spread, her landlady turned her out; no one would give shelter or employment to one who had betrayed Whitby sailors to the press gang. In the end, privation and exposure drove her mad, and Crazy Polly, as she

became known, wandered the moors telling any travellers she met that she was waiting for her lad to come home.

For Hester and Dorothy there was a different, happier, ending. After three years of patient waiting, the day came when they once again saw their lads return up the track from the beach. Inevitably they were changed; they had seen dreadful things and been wounded, but they had survived and come home to tell the tale, unlike so many of their comrades.

'You want the wedding straight away?' gasped Mrs Mossburn. 'Eh well, I'm not sure how your father will tek it ...'

3

HOLY FOLK

KING EDWIN AND THE TEMPLE OF WODEN

Goodmanham

A young man is sitting on a stone in the dark. He is a prince, heir to a kingdom, but that is no comfort to him for he is on the run from his enemies and one of his few friends has just told him that King Redwald, with whom he has taken refuge, has been bribed to poison him.

He sits with his head in his hands, near to despair, when a slight sound makes him look up. A stranger has appeared from the shadows. The young man stiffens, but the stranger approaches in a cheerful fashion, his hands held up to show his friendly intent, though his face is hidden by darkness and his hood.

'What is a young man like you doing sitting out here in the cold when everyone else is in bed?'

'It's no business of yours what I do!' retorts Edwin.

'Is it not? And yet, Prince Edwin, I know very well what troubles you. Tell me, what reward would you give to the person who could free you from your problems?'

Edwin has heard men make unlikely boasts before, but when you are young, hope quickly replaces despair. 'I have no treasure as yet,' he says, 'but I would reward such a man in any way I could.'

The stranger smiled. 'And what if that person were to promise that you would recover the kingdom of Northumbria, defeat your enemies in battle and enjoy greater power than anyone who has ever ruled the English nation?'

Edwin stares at him. Surely he is asleep and this is a dream! Or could it be a vision?

'If one man could do that then I would never cease to honour him my whole life!'

The stranger reaches out his hand and lays it on Edwin's head. 'Then let this be the sign between us. Remember this and keep your promises!'

Edwin bows his head in acceptance, but when he looks up again, the stranger is gone. 'A god has surely visited me!' he thinks. 'Thor perhaps or Woden himself!' His heart is filled with an unlooked-for happiness.

'Edwin! Edwin! The queen has done it! You can sleep safe!' His friend, Lilla, is running towards him with a look of joy on his face. It seems that Redwald has, at the last minute, been persuaded by his wife not to accept the bribe Edwin's enemies have offered for killing him.

In the days that follow it seems that not only has Redwald decided not to betray his guest, but that (perhaps out of guilt) he is going to support Edwin's claim to the Northumbrian throne. Almost overwhelmed by the sudden reversal of his fortune, Edwin finds himself at the head of an army marching north against his enemies. Fortune sits on his helm. In a year those enemies are dead on the battlefield and he himself is at last proclaimed king.

Much needs to be done in Northumbria because his predecessor was a cruel and rapacious man who has ravaged the kingdom. However, the one thing that Edwin's new councillors agree on is that the king must marry and provide himself with an heir as soon as possible. Edwin has already been married, his first wife dying young, but he is keen to obey his council, especially now that, as a king, he can ask for the daughter of another king. During his exile he saw the daughter of the King of Kent, Ethelburgha, known as Tata, and was instantly taken with her beauty and calm wisdom. He will marry her.

Edwin sends an embassy to Kent asking for Tata's hand, but the reply he receives suggests that there is an apparently insuperable obstacle: she is a Christian, while Edwin and the Northumbrians worship the old gods. Edwin and his councillors look at each other and shrug their shoulders. What's the problem? Why can't all these gods get on together? King Redwald has a temple with altars to both Christ and Woden in it.

The Christians are far too touchy, thinks Edwin, but he will placate them. He sends messengers back. Of course Tata can worship in whatever way she likes, he says; he'll never interfere. Can she bring priests with her? Of course! As many as she likes — as long as they keep their heads down and don't upset the locals.

Tata comes, bringing Christian attendants and servants as well as priests. She even brings a bishop, Paulinus. Local people grumble but the newcomers seem unthreatening enough, although there are occasional scuffles between them and Edwin's house carles. These are mostly limited to a bit of horseplay and name-calling: 'Accursed demon-worshipper!', 'Effeminate Christ-eater!', and so on. Only to be expected, say the king's councillors philosophically; they are happy because, despite the difference in religions, Tata and Edwin are getting on well and she is pregnant already.

Bishop Paulinus, meanwhile, is trying to explain Christianity to the nonbelievers. He has his work cut out. These new ideas seem very strange to people who've never even given much thought to their own religion. The gods are there to bring you luck in battle and fertility to the fields and your wife.

You make offerings to them to gain their favour and you go to their festivals to keep them happy. The ancestors believed in Thunor, Woden and so on, and they must have been right or they wouldn't have succeeded in taking so much land from the Britons.

Edwin, however, is a different sort of man, a thinking man with a keen interest in ideas. Already people remark on his strange habit of going off on his own to think about things. He loves his wife and spends a lot of time talking to her. He likes Paulinus too, whom he finds to be a courteous and well-informed man, with a genius for impassioned debate. Time and again the bishop urges the king to abandon his old gods and follow Christ. Wouldn't he prefer a bright heavenly future instead of the gloomy vagueness of the old religion's underworld? Wouldn't he sooner have the glorious son of God fighting on his side than untrustworthy demons?

Edwin is uncertain. He is a man who takes his time and considers all options. He understands that he is only king as long as the people and his war-band support him. Anglo-Saxon kings have short lives. Already his faithful Lilla has lost his life protecting him, throwing his body in front of the knife of an assassin. If he changes his religion he might have the help of God, but he might also offend his own people, whom he genuinely cares for. Then, too, this Christianity is very demanding. Priests seem to be able to interfere with every aspect of your life from council chamber to bedchamber. How does Paulinus know with such certainty that he is right?

Edwin tosses and turns at night. He goes off into the woods to think, but he cannot decide. Then one day, as he sits alone on a little hill near his summer palace in the Wolds, he sees a man coming towards him. The sun is in his eyes and he doesn't recognise him at first.

'Paulinus?'

'My son, what is a great king like you doing sitting here all alone?' The bishop approaches Edwin and, seeing the king so melancholy, he places his hand gently on his head in blessing. Edwin gasps as if he has been struck, remembering, for the first time in ages, that night in King Redwald's court, the promises he made.

'Paulinus? Was it you? Was it you that night?' He leaps up and seizes the bishop by the shoulders. Paulinus is a little alarmed. 'My lord, you are not yourself. Shall I send for your servants?'

'You do not remember that night in Redwald's court?'

'What night, my Lord?'

'You have no memory of it? Then it must have been a vision, but if so it was a true vision, for here am I, King of Northumbria. I made a vow that night, Paulinus, and I hold myself bound by that vow. My doubts are resolved. Do not worry anymore; I shall follow your advice and become a Christian.' Here Paulinus falls to his knees in thankful prayer. 'Oh, don't rejoice too soon. I cannot force my people to convert. Still I shall do what I may. I shall summon the Witengemot and ask them to consider the matter.'

The Witengemot is the body of senior male advisers who debate and decide things for the people. The king can influence them, but in the end he usually has to go along with their decision. Now, gathered together at the king's command, they consider his question, 'Should Northumbria become Christian?'

Paulinus speaks first, laying out as simply as he can the fundamentals of Christianity: how his God sent his only son to earth to take away the sins of ordinary people and how if they were to follow him they would be protected from Hell and from their enemies and go to a lovely place called Heaven when they die.

When he has finished, various members of the Witengemot stand and give the assembly the benefit of their opinions. Some raise questions. Wouldn't it result in the king in Rome (as they call the Pope) becoming their overlord? Wouldn't the fighting spirit of the young men be weakened by following such a man as this Christ, who, after all, was defeated and killed ignominiously?

Some strongly reject Christianity, saying that the whole thing is a Kentish plot to undermine Northumbria with foreign ideas and, anyway, how do we know that all those miracles the priests talk of really happened?

Some, rather confused, are worried by the rumour that Christians will have to consume real human flesh and blood in the sacrament.

The sun moves around as they speak and the shadows begin to lengthen. Rooks fly overhead, calling, and far away cowherds begin to drive their cows home for milking. After many men have spoken, Coifi, the High Priest, stands. He is an important man, one of the king's relatives. He supervises the rites of Woden in the great temple nearby. He is younger than the king, magnificently dressed, hung around with many jingling amulets.

'O King,' he says, 'I have heard what everyone has said and it is my opinion that we should seriously consider accepting this new religion.' A ripple of surprise runs around the assembly. 'Listen, I have been High Priest of Woden for years; no one has shown him more honour than I have and yet what has he done for me? There are many men around you, King Edwin, who have received from you more honour, gifts and higher positions than I have. Surely this wouldn't be the case if the old gods had any power?'

Many nod in agreement, remembering prayers unanswered.

Finally, slowly, one of the king's oldest and wisest councillors arises. 'My Lord, it seems to me that we here on earth know very little about life. We are like a sparrow that flies through the mead hall on a winter evening. It flies in from the dark storm into light and warmth and music, but after a few minutes of comfort it flies out again into the darkness. Our lives are very short, and what comes before, or happens afterwards, is hidden from us. If this new religion can reveal more about these things then it seems only wisdom to follow it.'

His words move the Witengemot. Men nod their heads gravely. Coifi rises again. He may be a priest but he still has the impulsiveness of youth. 'Are we agreed? Do you all say aye?' He looks around challengingly at the old men.

'Aye!' say most of them. The king nods. Paulinus utters a silent prayer of thanksgiving.

'Then,' says Coifi, 'let us begin now. Let us burn the old gods and their temples for once and for all. I am the High Priest; it is only fitting that I begin it. I shall destroy the temple of Woden with my own hands!'

Others begin to be carried away by the excitement of the moment. They start to shout 'Down with the gods! Down with the temples!'

'O King,' shouts Coifi. 'Give me a stallion! Give me a spear! And I shall complete what we have begun.' These two things no priest of the old gods should touch. The king nods. Men run and soon return with a snorting black stallion and a great war spear. His amulets clashing, Coifi leaps on to the stallion's back, making it rear and strike out with its forefeet. People jump back. He catches the spear and brandishes it.

'Who will come with me?' he shouts. 'Bring fire!'

Many run for their horses; other run to the cooking fires and seize burning brands. Soon a large gathering on foot and on horse are streaming towards the hill where the great temple of Woden stands. It is surrounded by gloomy trees, its painted wooden walls, inlaid with gold and ivory, are cunningly carved with figures and animals that seem to move in the wavering light of the torches, Men begin to feel fear but Coifi rides up to the doors and kicks them open. The stallion backs and shies, snorting with fear at the sudden smell of blood and burning offerings. It will not enter, but Coifi levels his spear and casts it with all his might into the shrine. Then, seizing a torch from the nearest man, he throws it after the spear. Others rush forward to add their own. In a few minutes the whole building is alight, blazing so brightly that it can be seen many miles away.

Maybe Edwin, Tata and Paulinus are watching; maybe they are praying. Edwin keeps his promises. He and his children and many of his people – though not all – are baptised. His realm becomes larger; his rule is notable for its peacefulness. But nothing lasts in this short life; sooner or later the sparrow must leave the mead hall. New enemies eventually succeed in killing Edwin; another king sits on the throne. Tata and her children return to Kent; most of the people of Northumbria return to the old gods.

But something new has happened. The world has changed subtly and the old ways are no longer the only ways.

HILD AND THE SNAKES

Whitby

A little band of travellers is picking its way through gorse and heather up the steep side of the Esk Valley. To their right the sun is going down behind the long flat line of the moors but they are weary after their long sea trip from Hartlepool and have no eyes for sunsets. Three of the party are women; the rest are men, carrying long staves for protection. All have burdens, even their leader – a woman, surprisingly – tall, thin and commanding. Despite the hill's steepness, she strides ahead, her eyes on the summit.

Hild, daughter of Hereric, niece of King Edwin, is a princess, descended from warriors. At the age of thirty-three she has fallen in love with the new Christian religion which seems to be sweeping the land. In the mead hall the harpers make heroes immortal with their song, but what is that to the glorious physical immortality promised to believers in Heaven? Life on earth is brief and hard; she has already outlived many of her friends and family. Baptised by Bishop Paulinus himself she has abandoned her home and all her privileges and possessions to become a nun and serve God.

She has seen from the first that what is needed are monasteries to establish the Christian way of life, and to spread learning. They are to be little beacons of light in this dark world of violence and worldly pursuits. To this end she has dedicated her considerable energies, arranging simple houses for monks and nuns, organising supplies, setting up timetables for worship and study.

Because of her noble birth the proud Northumbrian thanes are prepared to listen to her, even when she asks for money or land. So far she has founded, or co-founded, three monasteries further up the coast and has now been given some land above the Esk, at a little place called Streonshalh. (After the Viking raids it will be refounded as Whitby.)

Workmen have been sent on ahead to begin raising the frames for some simple wattle and daub huts, but as Hild reaches the top of the cliffs she sees with dismay that little has been done. There is a rough shelter, hardly big enough for her party, but no sign of monastery buildings.

She looks around and calls as the rest of the travellers come up panting, throwing down their burdens. Out of the shelter comes a grimy man who keeps glancing about him nervously. Hild can be gentle and kind when she chooses, but she is also a princess, used to having things done, and she is not happy.

'Where are the workmen?' she demands. 'Why have the houses not been started?'

The man stares at his feet and stammers one word, 'Worms!'
'What?'

'Worms – snakes – my lady; the whole place is infested with worms – evil, poisonous worms! The men all ran away on the first day.' Even as he speaks one of the other women begins to scream and leap back as a huge black snake, of a kind none of them have ever seen before, slithers towards her, its eyes glinting in the last rays of the sun. Two of the men hit it away with their staves.

'Hmm!' says Hild. 'We'll see about that. Well, there's nothing can be done until tomorrow. We women will spend the night in this shelter. You men will have to sleep outside, I'm afraid. Fortunately it's not cold.'

'But the worms, my lady—'

'Snakes sleep at night, man! Surely you know that! Herulf, get a fire going. Adhelm, break out the provisions. We nuns are going to thank God for our safe arrival.'

No one sleeps well that night and long before dawn Hild is on her knees, praying that the snakes be driven out of the land.

'O Lord, you gave your servant Patrick the power to drive the snakes out of Ireland, your servant Hild begs that you give her the power to do the same in this land.'

As the dawn breaks she can see that her prayer has not yet been answered; out of every crack and cranny come snakes large and small. They writhe and hiss, warming themselves in the morning sun. No monastery is going to be built while they remain.

Hild is filled with fury. These things have been sent by the Enemy of Mankind to frustrate the establishment of God's worship. She has to overcome them. She calls for a whip. No one has one, but the man who met them the night before volunteers to get one from the village. It is some while before he returns, by which time the snakes, increasing in numbers all the time, have driven everyone, even Hild, into the shelter. Every so often the men make a sortie and kill some, but there are always more and more, roiling and coiling on the headland, more and more coming all the time. It is uncanny; it is horrible; an evil mind seems to be driving them on and their hissing fills the air.

Hild remains unafraid. 'Where is your faith?' she demands. 'God protected Daniel in the Lion's den and He's not going to leave us helpless. Ah! My whip!'

She takes the whip from the sweating man and goes outside.

'Listen to me, Creatures of Hell! I am Abbess Hild come to found a new monastery to the glory of God. In His name I bid you depart! Go to whatever place is appointed to you!' Then she cracks the whip and begins to hit at every snake she can reach, trying to snap off their heads. The effect is immediate: the snakes hiss even louder, rearing up in a threatening manner. Some are as tall as she. None dares strike out at her, however, and she, unafraid, strides forward among them, cracking her whip. Suddenly their nerve seems to break; they begin to turn tail and flee. Soon a writhing carpet of snakes is moving slowly towards the cliffs. Hild does not falter; cracking her whip as though she is driving cattle, she forced the snakes to the cliff edge. They begin to fall, curling up as they do so.

By the time the sun has fully risen there is not one single snake left on the headland. They lie, curled in death, on the rocks below. Hild's monastery can now be built without fear.

In time it becomes famous; wise men, holy teachers, kings, bishops come to visit Mother, as Hild is known, and for a time it does indeed become a light in the darkness of a violent time.

Below the cliffs the dead snakes, still tightly coiled, sink into the earth, but so near the surface that they can still be found by those who look carefully. We call them ammonites, but their older name is 'Hild's Worms'.

CAEDMON

Whitby

A feast is being held in a house near Streonshalh. All the local people have been invited, including the abbey's lay servants. Everyone has eaten and drunk well. Now they are leaning back against the walls, chatting and waiting for the entertainment to begin. Smoke rises from the central hearth and hangs in a motionless cloud just below the thatch.

Now the host produces a battered harp and hands it with courtesy to his chief guest. The old man tunes it. People nudge their neighbours, and up and down the room there are calls for silence. Soon all is quiet except for the crackling of the fire. After a few polite words of thanks to the host, the old man begins. He sings of the great fight at Malden and his audience smiles in reminiscence as the familiar tale unfolds, murmuring agreement at the well-known heroic words:

Mind should be the harder, heart the keener,
Courage should be the greater as our strength weakens!

In a lowly place near the door sits a middle-aged cowman, Caedmon. His mind is stirred by the grand words. How wonderful to be able to create a poem like that! How clever its maker must have been! He leans forward to hear more, but the old man has finished and, with a smile and a nod at the applause, is handing the harp to his neighbour. The big man thinks for a moment, strums a few ragged chords and launches into a bawdy song. Released from the emotion of the first song, men laugh and stamp their feet.

Slowly, inexorably, the harp moves down the line of men, each taking his turn to entertain the rest. No one refuses because there is no one who doesn't know at least one song – except Caedmon, squirming on his bench. His friends grin and exchange glances as he rises, mutters something about having to relieve himself, and slips out of the door into the star-lit night. Once again he is red with shame at his inability to sing, or even to remember a verse. Angry at what he sees as his own stupidity he stumps off back to his cow-byre, where

he sleeps on a pallet in the room above the cattle. He flings himself down and pulls his cloak over his head, biting back tears of humiliation.

In the middle of the night a dream comes to him. A man in white stands beside his bedside calling his name, 'Caedmon! Caedmon!'

'I am here, master,' says Caedmon, sitting up and rubbing his eyes in confusion. 'Is it morning?'

'Caedmon, sing for me!'

'I, master? I cannot sing.'

'You will sing for me. Sing!'

The word 'SING!' rings in his ears; it grows louder and louder – no, not louder, clearer; so clear that he can hear all the overtones that make up the sound of the word. He can almost see them, spreading out like ripples; they are becoming rainbows, dancing in his eyes, spiralling down through his ears, sound becoming colours. The colours fill his world, spinning and interweaving like twining plants. They swirl around him, closer and closer; now they are becoming words – words, words, falling through his head in patterns, his head full of patterned words, the whole world broken up and rearranged into patterned words, pulsing with the rhythm of verse.

For the first time in his life, Caedmon the Stupid, Caedmon the Tongue-tied says, 'Master, what shall I sing?'

'Sing about Creation!'

And he does! The words pour effortlessly from his mouth, shaped and weighted with the strong rhythms of the verse of his people:

Now let us praise the Guardian of Heaven's Kingdom,

The Lord's might and purpose,

The works of the Heavenly Father!

He established each wonder from the beginning thus:

First, shaped for the children of Earth

Heaven as a roof, Holy Maker,

Then, Mankind's Guardian, Eternal Lord

Founded Middle-Earth, a fold for the folk.

When he wakes in the morning Caedmon lies for a moment staring at the sunlight streaming through the cracks in the daub walls. He can hear the cattle moving quietly below him. Then he remembers his wonderful dream; how vivid it was! He expects it to fade away as ordinary dreams do, but, no, he can still remember the poem. Cautiously he repeats the words to himself. It seems to him, inexplicably, to be really quite good! What is more, he can think of more verses he would like to add. Words buzz in his head as plentifully as bees in a hive. Somehow, by some miracle, he, Caedmon, an uneducated cowherd, has become a maker. He is filled with delight at the wonder of the world and its creator.

Soon news of his dream and miraculous gift reaches his master, the reeve, or estate manager, of the monastery, a man who has known him for many years. Caedmon finds himself humbly reciting his verse to him, watching the man's eyes widen with wonder. That very afternoon the reeve takes him into the monastery itself, where he has never been. It is a collection of long low buildings, built of logs, wattle and daub, thatched with straw. Caedmon is frightened and awkward; the men and women here are holy, he knows. They are not like ordinary people because they pray day and night. Local folk say that they can do magic because some of them can read Latin and write runes on parchment. Once Caedmon saw a wonderful page a monk had made, all black shapes and gold.

Somewhere in this place lives Mother, the great and saintly Hild, who banished the snakes. Men say that she is so holy that birds will not fly over the monastery, being unwilling, out of respect for her, to soil her dwelling.

Caedmon hangs back, but the reeve lugs him along, scratches on a door, and, when they are told to enter, pushes him through into a small hall. A tall, thin, elderly woman,

sitting by a window at one end of it, looks up from a book
set on a little reading desk. Her face is pale and lined, but her
keen eyes, thinks Caedmon, seem to look into his very soul,

'This is Caedmon, Mother,' says the reeve. 'The man I told
you of. Please listen to his words and, even though he knows
no Latin, you will see that God has truly visited him.'

Hild stares at Caedmon almost fiercely, then, seeing his fear,
she smiles reassuringly.

'Do not be afraid,' she says. 'Sit here on this stool at my side
and tell me all about your dream.'

When he thinks about it, later, that afternoon with Hild seems
even more unreal than his dream. He had told Hild the whole
tale, and then spoken the verses, adding the new ones he had
made. When he was finished Hild had praised him with tears
in her eyes, saying that an angel had truly visited him. She had
asked him whether he would not like to be ordained a monk
himself and spend his days making verses for God. He had
been stunned. 'What will the beasts do without me?' he had
asked her, wondering, but she had only laughed and told him
that there were plenty of cowmen but very few true poets.
Remembering her words, Caedmon is filled with a strange
new feeling: he supposes that it is joy.

For the rest of his life, Caedmon lives in the monastery as
a fully ordained monk. He makes many verses on Biblical
subjects in the Anglo-Saxon tongue, a new thing in a church
which uses Latin for most occasions. Monks and nuns
remember them easily because they are in their own language; he even has the pleasure of hearing that some of his
verses are recited respectfully in the mead hall. No one thinks
to write them down, however, because, though they are

greatly admired, they are not in Latin, the proper language for holy things.

Caedmon dies in time, well-loved and respected. Vikings ravage Streonshalh and destroy the monastery. In time the few lines above are all that remain of the verse of the cowherd who is now regarded by many as the father of English literature.

A MIRACLE TOO FAR?

Beverley
East Yorkshire folktales are more about people than dragons or fairies. Being practical is highly regarded and there is a natural downbeat attitude to most things – especially politics and religion. The following story gives a very cynical explanation for some of the miracles of St John of Beverley, East Yorkshire's most famous saint.

The Scots were being a problem again. They were helping the Vikings who had been driven out of York. If their collaboration were to succeed then King Athelstan's status as the first king of all England would be in peril. It was time to teach the Scots and their King Constantine a lesson. Grimly Athelstan marched his army north.

In Beverley monastery the abbot, Wulfstan, was discussing news of the march with his cellarer, Godrulf.

'He'll be bound to stop at Lincoln,' he said glumly. 'I expect he'll rest in the monastery there. He briefly stopped here once, do you remember? Never stopped praying.'

'Hmm,' agreed Gudrulf, grasping the abbot's train of thought immediately. 'He gave us a big gift. Pity we've spent it all.'

'We could just do with a bit of royal patronage. The refectory roof leaks like a sieve.'

'Trouble is,' said the cellarer, 'Beverley's not exactly on the way to Scotland, is it? I mean, he'll come up Ermine Street from Lincoln to York, won't he?'

'Unless–' said the abbot, tapping his nose.

'Unless?'

'Unless he happens to hear about a particularly holy saint somewhere else, my son.'

'Somewhere like Beverley, father?'

'Could be. Could be. Ever done any dressing-up, Godrulf?'

Athelstan's army was just arriving at Lincoln. The ancient walls of the town echoed with the sound of marching feet and the natives began to run out with things to sell. Just before the army reached the gates, however, it was met by a group of pilgrims. They were bareheaded, sandaled, dressed in blue, with leather bottles hanging from their leather belts and they were singing psalms lustily.

King Athelstan, always keen on religious matters, sent one of his men to ask who they were. The answer he returned with interested the king immediately.

'My Lord, they say that they were once broken men, lame or blind or crippled. They have travelled as pilgrims to many shrines all over the country seeking healing, but it was only when they reached the shrine of St John at Beverley that they were finally cured. Now they are returning home, rejoicing!'

Warriors were not afraid to cry in those days: the king's eyes filled with tears of happiness. 'So many!' he murmured, 'God's grace has been shown to so many! I remember visiting this shrine of St John once, before I became king, but, fool that I was, I did not then recognise its special holiness. Bring these pilgrims before me.'

Soon the pilgrims were telling him tales of their amazing cures, mentioning in passing, the particular holiness of the Beverley monastery. Athelstan pressed gifts on them. Then he sent for his lieutenant. 'Larwulf! I have it in mind to visit this shrine of St John to ask the saint's blessing on our campaign.' Larwulf looked aggrieved. 'But my Lord, the army—'

'My thanes will do as I command. And in any case the army will march on to York tomorrow as planned. You and I will ride with a small company to Beverley this very night.'

'But it's late, my Lord and the horses are tired.'

'Well, first thing tomorrow then!'

Abbot Wolfstan heard the glad tidings not long before the king's party arrived. He did a little dance, shouted 'Yes!' and punched the air. Then he sent the monastery servants flying around preparing a great feast. When his guest arrived, however, he received him with all the sober decorum that the abbot of such a holy place could be expected to offer.

Athelstan was a big scarred veteran with the heart of a wolf and the soul of a dove, always up for a battle, but longing equally for peace. He was an undemanding guest, used to going without, on whom the feast was wasted. The abbot, seeing his genuine devotion, felt a little ashamed of his own duplicity.

'Still it's for the good of the monastery,' he told himself.

At midnight the whole community processed to the abbey church to pray. After the service the king drew his sword and, kneeling, he laid it on the altar, next to St John's tomb, vowing that if St John and God allowed him to return victorious to claim it he would give rich gifts to the abbey.

At dawn the next day he his party left to join the army at York. At sunset Godrulf and the other 'pilgrims' mysteriously returned to Beverley, well pleased with themselves. Until, that is, the abbot sent them off again. North this time.

King Constantine was camped by a river with his allies, Olaf Guthrithson, Viking King of Dublin, and a couple of Welsh kings. Their joint army was considerable. Athelstan's army arrived too late in the day to cross the river and fight, but the king gave orders for the men to camp for the night drawn up in line of battle. His own tent was pitched nearby. The army settled down, knowing that the next day would decide the fate of England, for if Athelstan were to be defeated, the kingdom would once again break apart.

Athelstan, his prayers said, fell into the light sleep of a warrior. At about midnight he suddenly awoke, his hand automatically reaching for the dagger under his pillow. In the dim light he saw a robed figure by his bed. It was an old man with white hair.

'Who are you?' demanded the king, silently cursing his guards.

'O King, I am he you asked for help. Your request has been granted! Lead your army across the river, O King, and you will have victory. Do not forget the solemn vow you made by my tomb or your sword on my altar!'

With these words the figure stepped backwards into the shadows and disappeared.

Athelstan lay still for a while, trying to gather his thoughts. Had that been real? A dream? A vision? He rose and called his guards.

'Did you see that old man?'

'What old man, my Lord?' The two guards looked at each other guiltily – there were serious penalties for sleeping on guard duty, but the unexpected discovery of a full wineskin had been too good to pass up.

'No, my Lord. No one has come past us,' said one.

'No one at all, my Lord. We've been watching all the time,' said the other, sweating slightly.

Athelstan was silent. Then he said, 'If you saw no one, then it must have been a vision.'

'A vision, my Lord? A vision of what?'

'Victory, my children! Heaven and St John are on our side! Fetch my armour!'

The very next day the great King Athelstan, first king of all England, defeated his enemies at the Battle of Brunanburh, a fight celebrated by poets for years afterwards:

The dark raven with hooked beak,
The pale toad, the eagle and kite,
The hound and wolf with brindled hide
Were long refreshed!

The king returned in glory to St John's shrine to regain his sword. He lavished gifts on the monastery. Furthermore he declared that any hunted person, criminal or otherwise, could claim the safety of sanctuary for a mile around the abbey church, now called Beverley Minster [for Beverley's curious sanctuary laws, see Notes]. Abbot Wulfstan was a happy man – the refectory roof would now be mended (and he had some long-cherished building plans that might now be contemplated).

As he was leaving the monastery, Athelstan passed a man in the courtyard. He stopped and stared at him. The man, a monk, pulled his cowl further over his face.

'You, father,' said the king, 'don't I know you?'

'I don't think so, my Lord. Born and bred in East Yorkshire, my Lord.'

'I'll remember in a minute – Ah! Now I've got it – you look just like St John – I saw him in my vision, you know!'

'Do I? Ah, yes, well – lots of people have noted my likeness to the saint – I'm – er – descended from the same family, you see. Family likeness, I suppose,' muttered Godruff.

'Oh, yes? That must be it then. You are blessed by the resemblance, I'm sure. Where's my horse?'

And so King Athelstan rode away happy while the abbot and the cellarer, exchanging small smug smiles, went to confession …

4

ODDITIES

GOOD VITTLES

Pocklington
Farm labourers in the East Riding were rather better paid and treated than their counterparts further south. They were a tough, stubborn lot, regarding themselves the equal of their bosses. The following is a warning to farmers to feed their hired servants properly. Being a Yorkshire tale it gives a practical, rather than a humanitarian reason: it's the best way of getting your money's worth out of them!

Pocklington was in the throes of the annual hiring fair. It was always held at Martinmas in November, brightening up a dreary time of year. Very respectable people stayed at home, but for the farm labourers like Billy Stubbs it was an opportunity to let their hair down at the end of a year's hard work. He squeezed his way along streets packed with strong young men and women in various stages of intoxication, laughing, shouting, fighting, pushing, groping, slapping. Booths selling all sort of solid fare from pies to pigs' trotters lined the road, and further out of town there were shooting galleries, Punch and Judies, freak shows and cheapjacks selling dodgy watches.

All around the outskirts of the town carts, horses, waggons and gigs formed a huge whinnying traffic jam.

Billy's own business, however, was with the real purpose of the fair: the hiring. It took place in the centre of the main street. East Riding farmers hired their farmhands for a year at a time, supplying bed and board as well as a wage. Most hands liked to move on to what they hoped would be greener pastures at the end of the year. The work was the same wherever you went so a change of scenery was important. They used to sing:

Good morning Mr Martinmas
You've come to set me free
For I don't care for Master
And he don't care for me!

The lads and lasses who lined up in the middle of the street held, by tradition, something to show what sort of job they were after: shepherds, a crook; cowman, a wisp of straw; dairymaids, a milking stool. The farmers walked up and down looking for strength, size and good health; it was, superficially, rather like a slave market without the chains. The weak and weedy were often left behind, jobless, in the muddy street.

Despite the appearance to the contrary, the power was not all on one side. Billy was not weak. He was a big strong lad who knew that he was prime stock, so to speak; getting hired would be easy. His only problem was (the most pressing one for farm labourers) how to choose from among those keen to hire him one who wouldn't stint on food. They called it 'having a good grub shop'.

He considered the smart clothes and big red faces before him. How to choose?

Someone outside one of the pubs was singing a warning song that made him smile, inwardly at least. It was a popular ditty about the awful food allegedly served by a mean old East Riding farmer:

> Now our owd measter to us did say
> There's a yowe [ewe] been dead for a year and a day
> Fetch 'er oop Bullocky, fetch 'er oop Sly
> We'll mek ourselves a bit o' rare mutton pie
>
> So we fetched t'owd yowe and laid 'er on table
> To mek mutton pie just as fast as we were able
> There was maggots hundreds, thousands, millions thick
> T'owd Bullocky were wallocking 'em off wi' a stick …

Billy had already put off several farmers he didn't like the look of or who had a reputation for meanness, but he'd have to make a choice soon. A kindly looking man now approached him. He was well but comfortably dressed. Billy took to him immediately.

'Is ta hiring?'

'Aye.'

'Work for me?'

'I will if you give me plenty!'

'Money or food?'

'Both!'

The man laughed. 'Ten shillin' a week and ma wife's the cook.'

'Done!' said Billy, 'I'll coom!'

The farmer gave him half-a-crown as 'fest' money. It was supposed to 'fasten' the bargain and you were supposed to give it back if you didn't take up the position – difficult if it had been spent in the pub!

Well, Billy went to the farm up in the Wolds, but he soon realised that he'd made a mistake. The farmer had married a new young wife with little experience of feeding workmen.

She gave them bread and cheese; plenty of both, but even so, not enough to support hard work. Billy couldn't go back on his bargain – ten shillings a week was good money. He had to find another way to change things.

One day the farmer was walking around his farm when he heard Billy singing loudly in the barn:

Bread and cheese, work as you please
Bread and cheese, work as you please.

At first the farmer thought it was some new song he hadn't heard before, but then he got to thinking.

When he'd finished thinking he went to talk to his wife. 'What have you been feeding the men?'

'Bread and cheese. What else?'

Now the farmer didn't like to criticise her to her face; after all they had only been married a short time, and the feeding of the men was her job, so he said, 'Well, I heard one of them singing "Bread and cheese, work as you please".'

'Well I never!' she said. 'And how did he seem to be working?'

'I peeped through a knothole in the barn so he couldn't see me, but I saw him and he was working as slowly as possible.'

'That'll never do,' said the wife. 'I'll try them with something richer.'

She was a good cook, just inexperienced, so next day she made a nice plum pudding and an apple pie. In the evening she was on tenterhooks to find out if the work had improved.

'Well,' said her husband, 'this afternoon I heard Billy singing "Plum pudding and apple pie, Do you work according-lye".'

'And was he working any better?'

'Summat better, but not crackin'.'

'Oh dear, I'd better think on.' So she did and next day she roasted a big piece of beef and made another pudding.

This time when the farmer rounded the corner of the barn he heard Billy singing:

Roast beef and plum pudden
Do your work like a good 'un!

'I think you've sorted it, love. He's workin' as hard as an 'oss,' he told his wife.

From that day on Billy and the others were fed with the best the farmer's wife could get, and when the next Martinmas hiring came around master and man parted well satisfied with their year's bargain.

SALTERSGATE INN

Saltersgate, near Whitby
If you drive past the Hole of Horcum beauty spot and down the steep bend known as the Devil's Elbow, you will see on your left-hand side a sad, dilapidated house, surrounded by scaffolding. It is, perhaps, involved in some legal or planning dispute, since it has been in a bad state for some years, but once it called itself the 'Legendary Saltersgate Inn' and was the haunt of smugglers and, if you will believe it, the Devil.

It was a dark and stormy night – no, really, it was – as dark and stormy as the pit of Hell. In fact, however, the Devil had nothing to do with this particular storm because he himself was suffering as he crossed the moors around the Hole of Horcum on his way to Whitby. No devil worth his horns wears an anorak so he was as wet and cold and miserable as someone who always carries Hell around with him can be. The rain sluiced (sizzling slightly), down the back of his neck.

As he rounded the corner of the Devil's Elbow he saw a light. He peered through the rain. Surely that was a house, or could it be an inn? It was still miles to Whitby.

'I'm completely knackered!' he said to himself. 'I'll see whether there's someone in that house who'll take pity on a poor old devil.'

As he got closer he could see that it was, indeed, an inn, a fine, welcoming coaching inn with busy stables, smoke billowing from the chimneys and jolly lanterns swinging in the wind on either side of the door. He could hear the sound of clinking tankards and jovial chatter. Over the door creaked the inn sign 'The Saltersgate Inn'. The Devil didn't care much for salt – people were always throwing it over their shoulders at him, for some reason – but in the rain the place looked cosy enough to tempt an angel. He pushed open the door and soon stood dripping in the entrance to the taproom.

'Good Lord, Sir!' said a rosy-faced barmaid, her eyes sliding, unseeing, over the Devil's horns and tail. 'Tha's wet as an 'addock! What a terrible night and thoo without tha great-coat! Thoo must be starvin' cold. Here, give me that jacket to dry and come over to the fire. Move up there, Harry, Will, let the poor gentleman in. Now Sir what can I get'ee?'

'Pint of porter!' gasped the Devil.

'Pint of porter it is and tha'll be wanting food as well, I guess. We've a nice chine of beef or how about mutton chops? There's a big party of Excise men in the Sun [all the rooms had different names], God rot 'em – not but what their money isn't as good as anyone else's – and they've et up all the ham and there's no fowls because of the party of vicars – was that a shiver, Sir? I hope tha's never catched a cold – in the Star – never known such folk for fowls as vicars – can't get enough of 'em – so what's tha fancy, Sir? I can get Nobs to lay a fire in the Lamb or thoo can eat in company here, just as thoo pleases, Sir.'

The Devil, who had dried off somewhat by the time the rosy barmaid had got to the end of this speech, smiled ingratiatingly.

'I'll eat in here – Betty, isn't it?' (She gasped with delighted surprise.) 'Mutton chops, I think, sweetheart, but could those pretty white hands bring me the porter first?' Betty, who was rather vain about her hands, felt herself blushing.

'And bring a pint for all these gents!' the Devil added. 'Something for yourself, too.'

Until then the men around him had been eyeing him with a certain hostility, but the atmosphere changed instantly. He was offered a seat and someone filled and held out to him one of the inn's long communal pipes. No one saw him light it, but, an instant later he was comfortably wreathed in smoke.

'Well, gents,' said the Devil, 'there seems to be a lot of custom at this inn. It's a lonely place, though. Is it normally so busy?'

'Lor' love'ee, Sir,' said Will, who sat beside him, 'didn't thoo see the toll gate? This is the end of the first stage from Whitby. Folk like to stay here and bait their horses. Then they go up the Devil's Elbow fresh as a daisy in the morning.'

'I'm surprised to hear that there are Excise men here,' said the Devil, noting, with an inward smile, the shifty look that passed over the faces of several of those around him. 'Surely they can't be looking for smugglers so far from the sea?'

There was a moment's uncomfortable silence.

'Well now, Sir, thoo's tret us like a gentleman, but before we answer that, we'd like to know where thoo stands on the Excise tax, free-traders [smugglers] and suchlike.'

The Devil leaned back and blew a smoke ring. 'Hm. Where do I stand on Excise? Well–' He contemplated his porter, thoughtfully. The men waited, exchanging glances. 'This is what I think – I think the king's rich enough already!' He raised the tankard. 'To the devil with Excise men! Here's a toast to jolly smugglers everywhere!'

All the men in the room raised their tankards and drank with great satisfaction – all but one, that is. A thin rascally looking cove crept out of the door when he thought no one was watching, muttering something about the jakes.

'That's Brown Jemmy, Sir,' whispered Will. 'He'll be off to report thy toast to the Excise men.'

'What care I? Damn his eyes for a tattle-tail! Another pint all round, Betty my sweet!'

Now that they knew his views the locals couldn't do enough for the Devil. They bought him drinks, listened open-mouthed to his stories and laughed uproariously at his disreputable jokes. The mutton chops were brought and consumed (though no one afterwards could remember seeing them being eaten). Soon the taproom noise level began to rival that of the storm outside. Betty was kept so busy that she started to look scarlet rather than rosy. In fact so noisy did things become that people in the other rooms were disturbed. The inevitable happened: the door to the tap room flew open and several burly Excise men barged in threateningly.

'Stow yer infernal racket!' one of them swore. 'Or by God we'll make you!'

A dangerous silence fell. Half the room got to its feet. Excise men and smugglers: two groups of sworn enemies faced each other. Then the Devil chuckled. 'Infernal eh? Well? What are you waiting for, boys?'

The melee that followed was in the finest bar room brawl tradition, all punches and flying furniture – much pleasanter to see than to read about. The Devil took no part in it but stood out of the way on a stool, guarding his pint and urging on the brawlers. Betty hid behind the beer barrels in tears.

The fight was at its height when there came an enormous banging so loud that it halted the brawlers in mid-punch. A bulky and impressive figure stood in the doorway, thumping the floor with his gold-knobbed stick. His broad hat was as black as night, his wig as white as snow, a huge gold watch chain stretched across his ample stomach, but it was the spotless Geneva bands around his mottled neck that made the combatants suddenly look guilty and surreptitiously drop their chair legs and bottles.

'Stow it, lads, it's the rector!'

Now you might wonder how a mere rector could have such an effect. It might possibly have been because of his holiness of life, but the more likely explanation is that he was also the local magistrate and could have had any of them thrown into gaol for a very long time.

In complete silence the rector advanced into the room, looking at each man in turn. Each wriggled away from his gaze. When he got to the Devil he stared hard. The Devil coughed and smiled weakly. The rector grew pale and then grew red. He raised his arm impressively, pointing. 'Are you all blind? Do none of you see who this is? Look at his horns! Look at his tail! Look at his cloven hooves! This man is the Devil!'

Immediately everyone could see it. Aghast they backed away.

'Avaunt, Satan!' shouted the rector. 'Leave this house and never return! Return to Hell where you belong!'

The Devil jumped down off his stool, 'Hang on a tick, old feller—'

'Get thee hence!'

'Lads! Lads! Put in a good word for me, won't you?'

The men stood stony-faced.

'But it's pouring! I'll get my death—'

'Go! In the name of Christ!'

Forced unwillingly through the silent crowd by the rector's powerful words, the Devil glanced around for an escape. As he reached the door he ducked into the passage and ran along it looking for a place to hide. He opened a door at random and found himself in a hot busy room, where a startled cook raised a protective ladle against him. The Devil looked around desperately. There was a fine peat fire burning on the hearth. He avoided the assorted cooking pots hanging over it and with a chuckle dived into the flames. 'No more rain for me, thanks!' he thought, settling himself comfortably.

The rector was just in time to see him jump. 'Aha! Now we have him trapped!' he chortled, waving his arms. 'I bind you, Satan, to remain in this fire for as long as it burns. In the name of Father, Son and Holy Ghost! Without your diabolical interference I may be able to bring some sort of God-fearing behaviour to this rabble!'

The Devil didn't reply. He knew that the fire couldn't burn forever. Sooner or later he would get out. He settled down to wait.

He waited a long time. A couple of hundred years.

The news that the Devil was trapped in the kitchen fire made the cook very unwilling to be around when he was released, and so she made sure that it was always kept well banked up. When she retired the next cook followed what had by then become a tradition, and so did the next.

The fire was still burning in my own lifetime, but the inn itself was deteriorating. At some time in the nineties it was closed, the tradition lapsed, the fire went out and – presumably – the Devil escaped. The sad state of the inn today suggests that he rather resented his long imprisonment.

THE FLYING MAN

Pocklington

England was in the grip of flying mania. Suddenly everyone wanted to see man (yes, it always WAS men) attempting to imitate the birds. Don't get the wrong idea: this was the 1730s and it was not exactly the dawn of human flight; no planes or even balloons yet, only very high church towers. Hardly a tower in the land escaped having a rope tied to its crockets, down which a gallant performer would slide with wobbly grace to the applause of the populace.

'No amusement was seen but the rope; walls, trees and houses were mounted for the pleasure of flying down; if a straggling scaffold pole could be found, it was reared for the convenience of flying' (William Hutton, *History of Derby*).

Men got together to lay bets on the probable survival of a particular performer. Boys abandoned their traditional leapfrog and knuckle-bones to beg, borrow or steal old pieces of rope to tie to local trees. Women shook their heads at the danger and the foolishness of men, though they were all there, staring upwards with their menfolk, their mouths open, when a Flying Man show came to their town. And what dangerous stunts those men invented! In Derby one offered townsfolk wheelbarrow rides from the top of what is now Derby Cathedral. He followed this up with an heroic flying donkey, whose little hooves were somehow fastened to the rope. (The rope broke, but no one, apparently, was killed, not even the donkey which had a soft landing on a spectator.)

This is how the flying was done: a rope was slung between two points, (one usually higher than the other) rather like a zip wire but looser. The performer was connected by straps or a board to iron rings strung on the rope and then, suitably attired in some sort of wings, 'flew' down fast from the high point. He would be slowed down (hopefully) by the rise of the rope to the second point where, to general acclamation, he would be safely caught.

It was a horribly dangerous thing to do, given the dubious hemp rope of the time and the often decayed state of church towers – several steeples were severely damaged. The life of the Flying Man was in the hands of whomever controlled the other end of the rope. Tension was vital: too tight and the rope would break; too loose and the Flying Man would hit the ground.

No matter! Crowds paid well, courage brought public esteem and ordinary life was pretty dangerous in any case. If you had a head for heights and the guts to do it you could earn enough money to live like a lord – temporarily.

Thomas Pelling, a Lincolnshire man, had done a fair few flights when someone suggested that he go to the big fair in Pocklington, a town on the edge of the Wolds.

'There's a grand church tower and lots of folk who'll pay well to see thee.'

Thomas decided to go. Pocklington Fair attracted many performers of different sorts who wouldn't have gone if it was not a lucrative venue. His daring flight was advertised in advance in the local pubs and interest was intense. On the great day a crowd gathered, big enough to gladden the heart of any performer.

Thomas slung his rope between All Saints church tower and the top of the Star in Market Street where it was wound around a windlass. A modern person would have run a few tests, got the tension right in advance, perhaps had a dummy run with a dummy, but this was the eighteenth century and in any case hemp ropes stretch unpredictably depending on the dampness of the air. For Thomas, the only certain way to tell whether his rope was properly tensioned was to use it. There were a few seconds at the beginning of his descent when he could make signs to the man at the other end to tighten or loosen the rope. Apart from that it was just luck.

Alas for Thomas!

Dressed as a bat, he waved to the cheering sea of faces far below and muttered his usual prayer.

'Good crowd,' he thought, 'should make some money here. Perhaps I'll buy Tommy a pony.'

An assistant fastened him to the iron rings with a strap around his chest and another around one leg. He would need his arms and the other leg for balance. Then, head first, he launched himself off.

Immediately he could feel that the rope was giving too much. He waved at the windlass man but either he was misunderstood or the man turned the windlass the wrong way in his excitement. The rope slackened still further and Thomas went – smack! – into the battlements at the eastern end of the choir. Screams and gasps from the crowd; men ran to disentangle him.

'He's still alive!'

'Thank God!'

But Thomas had fractured his skull and, after two days, he died.

Many a daredevil entertainer has been killed in an accident and been forgotten; Thomas Pelling, however, lives on in Pocklington myth. His splendid gravestone in Pocklington church, which declares that he is buried where he fell, still attracts interest and the lack of any details of his personal life provides a space for artistic speculation. The Flying Man Festival is held in his honour and volunteers abseil down from the church tower for charity in remembrance of his disastrous flight. All manner of other air-related activities, from flying teddy-bears to gliding, reveal that, in Pocklington at least, there has been no loss of interest in aerial excitements.

The White Powder

Possibly Willey Howe

A courtroom. The judge, a jolly, down-to-earth, huntin' sort of cove, is – much against his will – investigating a man accused of witchcraft. The judge considers witch-hunts things of the uncivilised past, but he can't dismiss the case out of hand because punishment for witchcraft is still on the statute book. Besides, the case has been brought by important local people. The accused is said to do miraculous cures by means of a white powder, a sure sign, say his accusers, of commerce with the Devil …

'Your honour, I'm a poor man, unlettered, but I have managed to provide meat and drink for my family by the white powder. I do cures, my lord, with the white powder. Where did I get it? Why from the fairies!' (Sniggers in court.)

'I am a poor man, but once I were even poorer. I were in deep distress, your honour, not knowing how to keep my bairns from starvation. One evening I were going home from the fields feeling right sad, when I met a woman. (More sniggering in court.) No sirs, she were not that sort of woman. She were a lady, a fair lady, with rich clothes. She asked

me why I were so sad and when I told her she said that if I followed what she advised then I could get me a good living. I said that as long as it were not wrong – meaning against the Bible, your honour – then I would do it. Then she said that, no, it were not wrong, but it were about curing sick folk and doing good. She said that I should meet her again t'following night, at the same time, same place.'

The judge, intrigued now, in spite of himself, asks him what happened.

'Well, Sir, I did as I was bid, and she came again and said it were well that I were on time, or I would have lost her favour. Then she took me to a little hill and knocked three times and the hill opened (gasps – and laughter – in court). And so we went in and it were a big hall – as big as the Guildhall, your honour – and in it a queen wi' a fine canopy over her and lots of fine ladies and gentlemen around her. My lady – I mean the one who had brought me there – presented me to her and she greeted me kindly. Then she told my lady to give me some of the white powder, which were in a box next to her, and teach me how to use it, so she did. She gave me a box full of it and bid me give one or two grains to any that were sick and it would heal them.

'What did we do next? Why, Sir, she took me out of the hill again and we went our ways.'

Here the judge, prompted by the righteous gentlemen who had brought the charge, asks whether the hall was dark or light. If it was dark, so the thinking went, then the place was probably Hell.

'Well, I don't know, Sir. Neither one nor t'other, much like this room.' (The judge smiles behind his hand.)

'How do I get more powder? Oh, that's easy! I just go back to the hill, knock three times saying "I am coming, I am coming!" at each knock and it opens up. Then I go to the

queen and she gives me more powder. (A babble of mixed dis-
belief and wonder.) It's true, Sirs, as I stand here. Why would
I lie? If any of you gentlemen would like to come with me,
or send his servant, I will take him to the very place and he
can see for himself that what I say is true.'

No one wants to look a fool by taking him up on his offer.
The judge sighs. He is now in a quandary. He thinks that
the accused is either a confidence trickster or a lunatic, but
he has to be careful as many people still believe in witchcraft, though that belief is waning. Fortunately there is no
evidence that any harm has ever been done by the white
powder – on the contrary – and so he is able to direct the
jury to acquit the accused. As he does so he mutters grump-
ily that if it were up to him he would whip him all the way
to his fairy hill …

Village Stereotypes

Fimber
It may seem odd in these days when people move around so much,
but in the past there was considerable rivalry between villages all
over England. Your own village was, of course, the best, where
the strongest and cleverest people lived, and your children would
adapt (and shout) hoary verses about the moral degeneracy or
idiocy of neighbouring villages such as:

> *Market Weighton*
> *Robert Leighton*
> *A brick church*
> *And a wooden steeple*
> *A drunken priest*
> *And a wicked people!*

Certain places might acquire a reputation for some particular characteristic: the Yorkshire village of Austwick in North Yorkshire, for example, has its carles: men famed for their stupidity (almost identical to the more famous 'Wise Men' of Gotham). In East Yorkshire, where every village showed its sturdy independence by having its own local words and pronunciation, the stereotypes were rather more nuanced. East Riding folk have a very dry sense of humour that can catch you out. Why were the folk of Nafferton, for example, said to 'shoe pigs?' A dig at gentrification?

Here is a little tale from Fimber, an extremely ancient settlement on top of the Wolds.

A York gentleman is riding through Fimber and sees three of its inhabitants lying at their ease on the village green. He stops his horse.

'Good day, gentlemen. I wonder whether one of you might show me the correct road to York?'

The three remain stretched out, but one of them raises his head and indicates the road with a jerk of his chin. The gentleman, somewhat baffled, tries again. 'Will one of you be so kind as to direct me to the nearest road to York?'

Silently another of the men raises a foot and points with it.

Amused by this apathy – or possible annoyed by the lack of deference – the gentleman says 'I will give one of you this half a crown if you will tell me which of you is the laziest!'

The first man yawns. 'Sir, I wouldn't thank you for your half-crown unless you throw it within my reach.'

Says the second, 'Sir, I will not thank you for your half-crown unless you get down off that horse and put it into my hand.'

The third has his eyes shut, but he mutters, 'Sir, I wouldn't thank you for it unless you put it into my pocket!'

Laziness or a sly retort?

THE OTHER SIDE

MEDIEVAL GHOST STORIES

There are a few Medieval folk stories from East Yorkshire, mostly written in verse in the fifteenth century. How well they reflect the actual stories told by local people is hard to know. However, M.R. James, the famous writer of ghost stories, made an interesting discovery while researching at the British Museum, which possibly gives us a better insight. He came across an ancient manuscript containing twelve ghost stories that seem much closer to real folk tales. They were written in simple Church Latin by anonymous monks from Byland Abbey and have the vivid raciness of first-hand accounts. You can almost see the monks listening, mouth open in amazement, pen in hand.

Although the tales are given a Christian gloss, the beliefs about the dead that they reveal would also have been understood by the tellers' Scandinavian ancestors.

For those not familiar with Christian belief, there are a few terms which may need explanation.

Excommunication is a punishment given by a priest to someone who has committed a really bad action and who refuses to repent of it. It cuts you off from the Church and, if not repealed by absolution (also given by a priest), it means that ultimately you will go to Hell. In these stories (contrary to the Church's official teaching), it appears to be popular belief that those who die unabsolved are doomed to walk the earth as ghosts unless they are lucky enough to find someone to help them.

Hell is for really wicked people.

Heaven is for really good people. With any luck we ordinary mixed mortals will get there when we have spent enough centuries in Purgatory being cleansed of our not-too-terrible sins in various unpleasant ways. This cleansing can be speeded up by the saying of Masses (a particular type of church service) and prayers by people who are still alive. You can leave money for Masses to be said to help your own soul – in the Middle Ages this was extremely common and was a nice little earner for the Church. In those days you could also buy indulgences, which were a sort of Get Out Of Jail Free card, supposedly authorised by the Pope. You could reduce the amount of time you were to spend in Purgatory by a certain number of years (depending on how much you paid).

And so to the stories …

The Baby in a Shoe

Byland Abbey

There was a man in Cleveland who went on pilgrimage to the shrine of St James at Compostella, leaving his pregnant wife at home. He travelled with a large party of other pilgrims for safety. Each of them took a turn keeping watch at night for fear of thieves.

One night they were all camped in a wood by the side of the highway. It was Richard's turn to stand guard. As he walked back and forth trying to keep awake he heard the sound of many hooves passing along the road. Wondering who could be travelling so late at night he silently crept through the trees, peering into the darkness.

As he reached the road he knew immediately that these were no living people. It was a riding of the recently dead; he had heard of such things. In the strange wavering light that they seemed to emanate he could see them clearly as they passed; men and women and children, silent and peaceful as the grave, all riding on various creatures. Some rode normally on horses, but others looked very strange, sitting on oxen, or sheep, or pigs; one man even straddled a goose.

At first Richard was mystified, but then he guessed that these animals were the ones that the dead people's relatives had given at their funerals as gifts to the Church; 'mortuaries' they were called.

'Folk wouldn't complain so much about having to give away stock to the church if they realised it was helping their dead like this,' he thought. 'I must remember to leave the friars a decent horse in my will!'

The dead passed him slowly and solemnly. The animals, even the small ones, carried their riders easily. Richard stood respectfully with his cap in his hand. Then, just as the last ones were disappearing along the road and he was turning to go back to the camp fire, he saw something small rolling along. It looked like an old shoe; a shoe with something in it. He followed it a little way, wondering what it could possibly be. Then he saw that inside the shoe was a tiny naked baby. He didn't dare touch it in case it harmed him, but he called out to it, 'Who are you and why are you rolling along like this?'

The shoe immediately stopped rolling and the baby lay in the dust looking up at him.

'I am no one.'

'No one?'

'I was born too soon and died.'

'Were you not christened?'

'No. I was buried swiftly in the dark earth. But,' it said, its big eyes pleading, 'you could help me if you wished.'

'Me? Why me?'

'Because I am your son. You could give me a name, father.'

When he heard this Richard was filled with grief and pity. He immediately took off his shirt and wrapped it around the baby. He held it close in his arms and with water dipped from a wayside ditch he christened it Richard. As soon as he had done this it seemed to grow. It cried out with delight, thanking him. He set it on the ground and now it could stand. With a last grateful look at its father it ran off after the departing dead.

Richard stood for a long time, thinking. He wondered whether his wife was alright and wished that he had asked the baby, but it was too late now. The shoe in which the baby had travelled still lay on the ground. At least someone had cared enough about the baby to give it something to cover it, he thought, picking it up.

Many months passed before Richard Rowntree returned home, his pilgrimage completed. To his great delight his wife was still alive and very happy to see him. He did not speak to her about the baby at first, but when all the neighbours had gathered that evening to welcome him home he asked his wife to bring him the old shoes he had left behind when he went on pilgrimage. She searched for a long time and then returned with only one shoe.

'I can't find the other anywhere. It's very strange. They were in the chest at the foot of the bed.'

'Is this it?' Richard brought out from his coat the shoe in which the baby had travelled.

The neighbours were confused. 'What's the big mystery about an old shoe?' they wondered.

One woman, however, turned pale. It was the local midwife. She burst into tears and fell on her knees in front of Richard. 'I'm so sorry!' she wailed. 'I buried the baby in the shoe. You see, it was premature and your wife told me to christen it – for as

you know, we midwives are allowed to do that if there is danger to a baby's life – but I was busy and didn't get around to it until it was too late. The baby only lived for a very little while, and when it died I buried it in the shoe. Your wife was ill and knew nothing about it. Forgive me!'

Richard then told the story of how the shoe had come rolling to him and how he had been able to help his son. Everyone was amazed and gave thanks to God, but his wife wept as she thought of the little child running after the dead down the quiet, dark highway.

The Tailor and the Wayside Ghost

Byland Abbey

A tailor named Snowball was riding from Gilling to Ampleforth on the edge of the North Yorkshire Moors one evening when he heard a sound like ducks washing themselves in a beck. Curious, he looked around but saw nothing other than a crow sitting on a tree. In the half-light it seemed particularly large. As he rode past the tree the crow fell to the ground, fluttering its wings as though it was in great distress. Snowball was a kindly soul, so he dismounted and went over to see what was wrong with it. However, as he got close he saw that sparks of fire were shooting out of its sides. He leaped back, terrified.

'For God's sake, don't hurt me, Master Crow! – I was just trying to help! I'm going! I'm going!' he cried. At the mention of God the crow shrieked and flew further off, but its bright eyes were still fixed on the tailor as he quickly mounted his pony and trotted briskly away.

He had not gone far before he was struck violently and knocked to the ground. He lay there stunned for a moment but when he looked up, the crow's beady red eyes, only inches away, were staring into his. Snowball was no coward: he jumped to his feet, backing and drawing his sword. 'Get away, Demon!' he yelled. He struck at the creature, but, as he told his fascinated neighbours later, it was like hitting a block of black peat.

Seeing that he could not damage the crow, Snowball once again jumped on to his fat little pony and urged it to something approaching a canter.

He rode away as fast as he dared in the gathering dark, but the creature he had encountered had not yet done with him. As he rounded a corner he found a great black dog with a chain around its neck standing in his way. The crow was a shape-shifter.

The pony stopped abruptly, digging in its hooves so that Snowball nearly fell over its head. He stared at the dog, wondering what he should do. He had heard of wandering spirits, sad ghosts who appeared to the living, begging them for help, but he had also heard of evil demons seeking to snare unwary souls. All conversation with the world of the Dead had its dangers, he knew; it could make you ill, or even bring about your death. And yet there was something so desperate about the creature's eyes that, despite his fear, he felt sorry for it.

'In the name of Christ,' he said, trembling, 'tell me your name and what your trouble is, then if I can help you in any way I will – provided you don't do me any harm, that is!' he added as a hasty afterthought.

The dog gasped and howled dreadfully, but at last it began to speak, not with its mouth (though that was so wide open that Snowball could see, with fascinated horror, right down its fiery throat) but with words produced deep in its stomach.

'My name is– [The monk who wrote this story down took a great deal of trouble not to reveal either the name of the ghost or what awful crime it had committed; presumably the name would have been recognised in Byland]. And I did some terrible things for which I was excommunicated by Andrew the Priest, so I must haunt this road, as you see. If you wish to help me, then go to him and beg him to absolve me. You must bury the scroll with the absolution on it in my grave. Then get

twenty Masses said for my soul and I shall be free. But be warned: if you do not return here in a week's time bringing the priest's reply then your flesh will begin to putrefy and your skin will weaken and fall from your bones! You must return here alone, at night, after you have buried the absolution and never reveal to anyone where my bones lie.'

'And where do they lie?'

'Look, here.' The dog went a little way into the woods at the side of the road and, sure enough, there was a green mound just visible among the trees.

'Alright I'll do it, but there's something you must do for me in return for my help,' said Snowball, greatly daring. 'You must stop haunting this road while I'm gone. Go away to Hoggebek.' [A long way up on the moors.]

'No! No! No!' wailed the ghost. 'I can't! It's too far!'

'Well then, go as far as Byland Bank; that's closer.' Sullenly the ghost agreed. 'And I need a promise that I'll be safe if I return here alone.'

The dog growled and sparks shot from its eyes, 'You will be safe ONLY if you return alone! But you will need to bring some extra protection with you because I am not the only ghost who haunts this road; there are two others, much more dangerous than me. One killed a pregnant woman; he appears sometimes like a thorn bush, sometimes like a fire and he cannot speak. The other was a corrupt priest who appears as a huntsman. Do not go near them. They are very evil! You must bring magic words with you; bring the four Gospels and a cross with the name of Jesus on it. Hold it over your head and you should be safe enough.'

Snowball drew a deep breath. 'Very well. I shall try to do everything you ask of me, but, tell me, can I look at the fire tonight when I get home?' [It was well known in those days that after meeting a ghost you had to be careful of looking at light or you would become ill. Some said that you should look at a fire before looking at candle light; others that you should see daylight before firelight.]

The ghost considered. 'You will be alright looking at a fire this time; next time it may be different. Now go!' But Snowball was still hesitating. 'What? Is there still more you want to know?' it growled.

'It's just occurred to me. What happens if the priest doesn't believe my story? He's only got my word that I've seen you.'

The dog sat back on its haunches and thought for a while. Then it said 'I once told Priest Andrew some things in confession that I have never told anyone else. He will remember them. I will whisper them to you. Lean forward.'

Snowball leant forward, closing his eyes so that he could not see the horrible dog coming closer. It put its foul mouth up to his ear and whispered into it. 'Will you remember?' it asked.

Snowball swallowed. 'I think it's very unlikely that I'll forget that!' he replied.

'Farewell,' said the ghost dog. 'Do not fail me!' The last Snowball saw of it was a fading eerie glow as it slunk away through the trees on its way to Byland Bank.

When the tailor reached home he collapsed and, despite what the ghost had said about the fire, was ill for several days. Then, as time was passing, he dragged himself to his feet and set off to York to find Andrew the Priest. The priest recognised the dead man's name, and remembered too the causes of his excommunication.

'I'm sorry, my son,' he told the tailor. 'He should have repented while he was alive. He was a bad man and deserves everything he's got. Besides, I'm not sure that it's possible to absolve someone after they're dead.'

Snowball pleaded with him, pointing out that the ghost would go on haunting the road if it wasn't absolved, and so finally Andrew agreed to consult a couple of other priests. They had a learned discussion together, arguing this way and that.

'It's my belief that this so-called dog is an evil demon, trying to get holy things to do harm with them!' declared one of the other priests. 'How do you know that this is really the ghost of the man you excommunicated?'

Then Snowball whispered into Andrew's ear the things that the ghost had told him. He went very pale and then said 'It's him, alright, brothers. Very well. I'll do it – it'll cost five shillings.'

Andrew wrote out the absolution on a scroll and gave it to Snowball who then arranged for Masses to be celebrated for two or three days. Exhausted he went home and slept like the dead himself.

In the morning he took the scroll with the absolution on it and rode back to the place where he had met the dog. It looked different in the daylight, but eventually he found the little green mound and buried the scroll deep in it. As he stood up he was suddenly overcome with fear. He looked around but saw nothing and nobody. Crows were calling and a chill wind blew. Was the ghost now freed? Snowball shivered and quickly went back to the road and his horse.

The week the ghost had given him was up next day, but his courage was fading fast. He hated the idea of meeting it again, especially at night. He asked everyone he knew what the best way of keeping safe was. They all agreed that he needed a circle of protection, such as a wizard might use. 'Take a cross,' they said, 'and draw a circle with it on the ground.' His local priest lent him a large cross with the signs of the Four Evangelists and the name of Jesus engraved on it. For good measure he also lent him four small reliquaries with remains of saints in them.

Thus armed, Snowball rode out into the night to meet the ghost. A neighbour had offered to go with him, despite the ghost's warning, but when it came to it he found a convenient excuse, and so the tailor was on his own.

When he arrived at the place, he dismounted and drew a hasty circle around himself and his pony with the cross. He placed the reliquaries at the four points of the compass. Then he hoisted the cross over his head and sat down to wait.

The moon rose above the trees and in its white light the tailor saw a goat trotting up the road. As it reached the circle it stopped as if it had hit a brick wall. Then it ran around the circle three times, bleating piteously. Then it fell to the ground and rose up in another form, a hideous skeletal form, like one of the Three Dead Kings painted on the wall of the parish church. It lurched and swayed far above the tailor's head, its horrible jaws creaking and snapping; its skeleton hands opening and shutting.

Snowball got to his feet, gripping his cross. His heart raced and his voice shook. 'Who are you? Tell me, I charge you in God's name!'

For a moment it looked as though the skeletal figure couldn't – or wouldn't – speak. Through Snowball's mind flashed the thought that perhaps this was really one of the more evil ghosts. What was he to do? Then a red light began to flow upwards through the ribcage, the bony mouth opened and a voice whispered the ghost's name. Snowball felt weak with relief, but he wasn't going to let his guard down.

'I've done what you wanted. Has it worked? Tell me, are you free?'

The form before him drew a huge sigh that made all its bones rattle.

'Yes!' it said, 'Yes! I am free!' At first it sounded as though it had not dared to say the words before, even to itself. Then its voice grew louder 'I'm free!' and louder 'I'm free!' It danced a little, put its horrible arms out to embrace Snowball, bounced off the charmed circle, put its skull back and laughed an echoing laugh. 'Thank you! Thank you! I was invisibly behind you when you buried the absolution – didn't you feel afraid? I was being tormented by several demons at the time, but the moment you buried that scroll they were forced to let me go. On Monday I and thirty other ghosts will attain Heaven, thanks to you. I shall at last find peace! There are no thanks great enough to give you.'

Tears came to Snowball's eyes. He sank down on to the ground. The ghost stopped his capering and looked concerned. 'You don't look well. Have you been ill?'

'I've not been right since I met you.'

'Hmm! – You must go down to the river and look for a broad stone. Lift it up and underneath you will find some sandy rock. Wash all your body and rub it with this sandy stone. You will be healed in a few days.'

Snowball thanked him, but now that his fears were allayed his curiosity began to grow. After all, how many people get to question a real ghost?

'Will the other two ghosts who haunt this road be freed too?'

'Oh no. One of them will never be freed. The other will have to wait for a boy to grow up.'

'And what about me? Will I go to Heaven?'

The ghost looked doubtful. 'Only if you give back that nice coat and hood you are hoping your friend will never ask you to return.'

'Oh, that's not fair! He left them with me when he went off to the war and I don't know where he is now!'

'Alnwick. Now you have no excuse.'

The ghost told Snowball several more useful things, such as which village to move to if he wanted to be rich and which one to avoid. Then he said that it was time for him to go. Snowball was strangely sorry to say goodbye; they had almost become friends.

The ghost's last words to him were, 'Remember, don't tell anyone where my grave is. Keep your eyes firmly on the ground on the way home, don't look at the fire tonight, sleep with holy writings under your pillow and you should be fine.'

Snowball did as he was told and, though he was once again very ill when he got home, he followed the ghost's advice and soon recovered. He moved to another village and became prosperous.

He made a point of travelling all the way to Alnwick and returned his friend's clothes and so, as he had first-hand experience of the terrible fate awaiting those who die unpurified, we must assume that when he died he went to Heaven!

THE THREE ROSES

Foot of the Wolds

Joe Davis was a miller by trade, as jolly a miller as you could hope to meet, the sort who would stand you a beer, tell you a joke and help you out in times of trouble. No one ever complained that Joe held back some of their flour or that he grumbled if you only brought one sack of corn to be ground. 'He's a right good'un!' was the general verdict. He had been looking for a mill to rent for some time, but hadn't been able to find one cheap enough. Mills were valuable property, often owned by wealthy men who wanted a good income from them. One day he heard of a mill at the foot of the Wolds that was being let at a ridiculously low price. He leapt at the chance and soon agreed a very good deal with the owner, a big bluff man who seemed delighted by his new tenant. He kept shaking Joe by the hand and saying 'Good man! Good man!'

The watermill stood in a hollow of the Wolds, surrounded by trees, but a delightful place on a sunny day. It was rather more dilapidated than Joe had expected and seemed to have been empty for some time, but his merry wife and three boisterous children – Joe's delight – soon filled its rooms with laughter and so, not being a man much given to deep thought, he didn't let it worry him.

It took a while to fettle the machinery, adjust the grindstones and repair the great waterwheel. Soon its comforting deep rumble was the background to their lives. Joe worked hard for a couple of weeks without going into the village, but a few neighbours dropped in to welcome the new family.

'Good luck, Mr Davis,' said one. 'Thoo must be a brave man!'

'Brave? How?'

'Doesn't tha know?' continued the neighbour, exchanging meaningful glances with the friend he had brought with him. 'Surely tha must know – surely someone must have said something!'

'Told me what?' Joe was growing a little annoyed. The neighbour sucked his teeth importantly and put on a long face. 'The mill's haunted!'

Joe laughed out loud with relief. 'Is that a'? Dinna tha worry, man,' he said. 'Me and me wife'll be a match for any bogles. I thought thoo was talking of woodworm!' The neighbours left in a huff. Others came visiting over the next week and said much the same thing, but Joe laughed it off.

'Trouble with the folks hereabouts, Mary,' he told his wife, 'is they've got too little to worry about.'

The mill showed no sign of being haunted that summer. The waterwheel rumbled, the stones ground sweetly, the children ran about happily and did NOT fall into the mill race, the sun shone and the birds sang. The miller sang too; he was a great singer with a sweet voice for such a big man. He sang at his work all day, particularly the song with which he had wooed his wife, 'The Rose of Tralee'. 'She was lovely and fair as the rose of the summer ...' filled the warm air as the children ran about.

When autumn came and the sun grew lower, the valley where the mill stood grew a little more gloomy; wind sighed through cracks in the dark timbers, leaves floated on the mill race. The miller's wife built up a good fire in the parlour. She had finally got it to her taste, shining with polished brass, smelling of polished wood; a comfortable chair for the tired miller and embroidered cushions on the long settle for the rest of the family. There were china dogs among the candlesticks on the mantelpiece and over it hung her pride and joy, a portrait of herself that the miller had had painted for their sixth wedding anniversary. It showed her standing in a garden in the blue dress she had worn at her wedding. In her hand she held three red roses, one for each of their children. The miller had paid a lot of money to the artist for it and it was held to be a very good likeness. For the miller's wife, however, it was a symbol of her husband's love; she valued it above all her possessions.

One evening the tea cloth had been drawn and the children were, for once, quietly reading by the fire. The miller's wife was sitting near them at her endless task of mending. The miller was in his chair, comfortably tired after a long day. His head sank back as he dozed off. For a while there was no sound but the distant rumbling of the waterwheel, the ticking of the longcase clock and the crackling of the fire. The miller's wife smiled to herself. It was one of those moments of peace that make up for all the drudgery of the day. She felt her own eyes begin to close …

Suddenly the miller started up wide awake, his eyes staring, his face as white as his own flour.

'What's up, love?' asked his wife. He did not reply but walked from the room like a man dazed.

From that day onwards Joe Davis changed. No longer the jolly miller, he never sang at his work anymore or laughed with the children. He moved around at his work with a distracted air and often failed to respond when people spoke to him.

His wife, shocked at the sudden change, tried at first to ignore it, giving him time to get over whatever trouble he was in, or at the very least get up enough courage to tell her of it, but his misery seemed to deepen day by day. No longer did the neighbours drop in for a chat when they brought their wheat to be ground. Instead they shuffled nervously and looked out the windows. When they spoke to the miller's wife they were unnecessarily solicitous; one woman even flung her arms around her in a big hug, and when she let her go there were tears in her eyes.

The autumn deepened into winter. Silence and gloom deepened in the mill. The children, increasingly disturbed, dawdled on the way home from school, putting off getting back to the cheerless place. They were not fooled by their mother's forced gaiety. The rumble of the waterwheel, which had always seemed so comforting, suddenly seemed threatening, a danger creeping towards them. Still the miller said nothing of his trouble. He avoided his family, finding unnecessary work to keep him out of the way.

Then one raw November night the miller's wife could bear it no longer. The millstones stood still, for there was little to grind at that time of year, but the fire in the parlour was burning as brightly as ever and the children were safely in bed. The miller had eaten his tea in silence and immediately gone out again, muttering something about the wheel. Usually his wife would had taken herself off to bed, but this night she waited up, determined to have it out with him. It was very late when she heard his slow step on the stairs – he who had always run everywhere – and then he was in the room, holding his cold hands out to the fire. He started when he saw her, but quickly she was between him and the door. Sorrow filled her as his drawn face turned towards her. 'Tell me! For God's sake tell me what's wrong? Have you lost all our money? Are you ill? Tell me, I must know!'

She saw him struggle with himself; then a curious blankness seemed to overcome him. 'It were the painting,' he said dully. 'It were the painting that night.'

'What night, love? Tell me!'

'That night when I suddenly started up. I had nigh fallen asleep. Then I had a vision or summat. I were still in my chair, but a sort of shadow of me rose up out of my chest, walked over to the fire and looked up at the painting.'

He paused and rubbed his forehead with his hands, 'Then he – me – the shadow – reached up his hand and touched the three roses in the painting – they were real somehow, as well as being painted and then ...' His flat voice ceased. Suddenly she didn't want him to go on.

'It were just a dream, love, nubbut a dream. No call to be frighted ...'

But he began again, drearily grinding out the words: '... He – I – touched the roses and they all faded. The petals just shrivelled up and fell off. Then he touched your blue dress and ... all the colour faded ...'

'No! Stop now!'

'... And your face went all grey and old. That's it, love. That's it. I made you all die.'

She couldn't speak. The spell of the horrible words struck her dumb.

'Go to bed, love,' said her husband, gently now. 'I have one more thing to do. Go to bed.' Without another look at her he left the room and she heard his boots once again going down the stairs.

Left alone she tried to shake herself free of fear. It was just a dream. What harm is there in a dream? 'Tha's a foolish old woman!' she told herself, but she felt in need of a cup of tea, nevertheless. The kettle hanging by the fire was never empty and soon she had brewed herself a strong cup. She sat in her usual place by the fire, but she found no peace there. Against her will she found her eyes straying upwards towards the picture. The three red roses were as beautifully painted as ever. There was a realistic drop of dew on one of them that she had always admired – though now she thought it looked more like a tear. The blue dress (torn up for dusters long ago, but lovely cloth) was unchanged, and her face–

Tea splashed as the cup broke on the hearth: staring out at her from her own face were eyes filled with a hideous malevolence; the painted lips now curved upwards in a mocking smile. At that very moment the miller's wife heard a voice, her husband's voice, singing outside. She ran to the window and flung it open. On the frosty air the song rang out, loud and clear.

She was lovely and fair as the rose of the summer

But 'twas not her beauty alone that won me

Oh, no, 'twas the truth in her eyes ever dawning

That made me love Mary

The rose of Tralee!

Then, with a great groaning of timbers, the millstones began to turn, shaking the house, grinding nothing.

See her standing there, Mary, the miller's wife, her hand on the window catch. Only one thought fills her head, one unreasonable but terrible thought – the children! The children are not safe!

She grabs a candle, blunders across the room (see the eyes of the portrait follow her!) and begins to climb the steep stairs to the children's attic. It is a long way up and, as in a nightmare, there seems to be a weight on her limbs that fights her every step. She has only reached the landing when she hears a voice from up above, her little boy's voice, drowsy with sleep, 'Oh Daddy, how cold you are! How very cold you are!'

She cannot move. The candle falls from her hand. Darkness covers her.

It is said that that's how they found her next morning, the men who came with corn to grind. She was sitting on the stairs, her eyes blank, her wits quite gone. In the attic lay her three children dead in their beds, not a mark on them.

'It's a blessing she knows nowt about this,' said one as they hauled the body of the miller out of the mill race. The other men shook their heads and said nothing.

The mill was torn down shortly after: no one would rent it.

The portrait was burned: who wants a picture of a grey woman holding three dead roses?

FIVE WHITE PEBBLES

York and Scarborough

May night is, as everyone knows, a chancy time of the year, the hinge between spring and summer, when all sorts of magic seep into our world from the Other. At that time it is possible to gather fern seed to make you invisible, you may see fairies or the spirit of your future partner; you can even look upon the faces of those doomed to die in the following year – if you are brave enough.

But beware! To do these things you must perform magical rites which may render you vulnerable yourself.

Once upon a time there was a certain knight just returned from fighting in France. He had been away for two years and longed to see again the face of his betrothed who lived in a great mansion near Scarborough. As his horse clopped the last few miles up the Great North Road into York, still far away from his beloved, he was surprised to meet bands of young people wearing green garlands and singing. They had flaming torches that startled the knight's horse. In an instant his sword was in his hand, the young people backing away in fear.

'What are you doing on the road at this time of night?' he demanded.

'Don't you hurt us, Sir! We're just going Maying.'

It was a moment before he stopped seeing them as an enemy ambush and remembered that that very night was May Eve. The young folk were May revellers, going to spend the night in the greenwood in honour of the season. He remembered how he and his love had also sometimes gone with them (long ago it seemed now, a time of innocence before he had been so scarred, so hardened by war). How joyfully they had leapt together over the Beltane fires with the others, never thinking that they would ever be parted.

As he saw the way the young couples were hanging on each other's arms, certain gloomy thoughts that had often haunted his dark nights in France welled up in his mind: suppose his betrothed no longer loved him? Suppose she had been false?

He shifted restlessly in his saddle and tried to shake the thought loose. If only he could see her NOW; if only she wasn't still so far away. Then, as he turned the horse's head toward York again, he suddenly remembered a piece of May night folklore from his childhood: it was said that if you dropped five white pebbles into the River Ouse on May Eve and made a wish, you would see the thing you most desired. It had to be done in a particular place, but he thought he could still remember where it was.

The horse trotted into the outskirts of York. Soon he and his master stood on the banks of the swiftly flowing river. Finding five white pebbles in the dark was much harder than finding the right place to throw them into, but the knight was filled with a feverish urgency and, though it took a long time, eventually he had all five in his hand. He closed his eyes and thought of his beloved, her beautiful chestnut hair, her small smiling red mouth. Wishing to see her with all his heart he throw the stones into the black water.

At first he saw nothing as he stared into the rushing river, but then it seemed to him that a whirlpool had started near the bank, and at its centre was a gleaming light, like the moon shining on silver. Slowly it grew until a still flat mirror seemed to lie before him, gently floating just above the water. He knelt on the bank to see more clearly and gasped as the well-remembered shape of his love's mansion appeared in the mirror, outlined against a moonlit sky. One of the windows was open: it was hers! As he looked closer the knight saw that a ladder had been set below it. Now something else was

happening; the slim figure of a young man was emerging
from inside the window and swiftly descending the ladder.
Another figure – a servant possibly – immediately came from
the shadows and quickly removed the ladder, hiding it under
some bushes. Then together the pair disappeared into the
blackness behind the mansion.

The knight staggered back from the water's edge. Rage flowed through his whole body so hard that he found himself panting like an enraged bull. The awful image of that young man in his jaunty cap swinging himself gaily out of the window filled his mind so completely that he could hardly find his way back to his grazing horse.

He flung himself on to its back, shouting some curse – he didn't know what – and dug his spurs into its sides. Soon it was clattering through Monk Bar carrying the knight on to the Scarborough Road.

Forty miles is a long way for a horse even when it is not tired. The knight's fury did not cease but it cooled to a hard cold hatred as he forced the exhausted animal towards his goal. The night passed, but long before the sun rose the dawn chorus was celebrating in full joyful voice the first day of summer. Drowned deep in his tormenting black thoughts the knight could not hear it. Bloody foam fell from the horse's jaws; it was staggering by now, held up, it seemed, only by its master's will.

As they approached the mansion the horse abruptly stopped, coughed and fell forward, dead. The knight was thrown clear but, unhurt, he leaped to his feet, drawing his sword. He swung it wildly as he ran towards the house whose stones were just beginning to glow golden in the dawn light. When he got closer he realised that the ladder he had seen in the water mirror the night before was once again against the wall and – look! – surely that was the same young man beginning to climb back up it!

The knight did not hesitate; in a few strides he had reached the foot of the ladder. The young man, whose back was to the knight, heard footsteps on the gravel, and he was just beginning to turn when the knight's sword stabbed upwards. He gave a cry and fell backwards into the arms of his murderer. As he did so his jaunty cap fell off, releasing plaited tresses of long bright chestnut hair. For a second the knight's tired brain could not deal with what he saw: the face, contorted with pain, that stared into his was that of his betrothed. He saw a second of horrified recognition flare in her eyes before they closed forever.

'What have you done?' screamed a voice at his shoulder; Richard, a long-time servant of the family, had rushed up and was now beating on his back with shaking hands.

'I thought–' stammered the knight, 'I thought it was – a – man ... I thought she ...'

Richard took his young mistress tenderly into his arms. Tears poured down his lined face. 'She just went to a May revel!' he cried. 'That was all. It was secret from her parents so she dressed as a young man! She remembered how happy she had been there with you! Oh Sir, what have you done?'

And weeping, he carried the dead woman away, leaving the knight alone with his bitter future.

The Fairy Cup

Willey Howe
The valley of the Gypsey Race has been a holy and magical place since the Stone Age. The race itself is a Woe Water, which only flows strongly in times of trouble, and it is adorned along its length with mysterious dykes and cursuses, the huge Rudstone and the great Neolithic burial mound called Willey Howe.

There was once a farmer riding home to Wold Newton on a winter's night. A light drizzle was falling and there was no moon, so his mare had to go slowly to avoid sliding into a ditch. The road led along the valley of the Gypsey Race, but the farmer wasn't thinking of disaster, only about the pleasant evening he had spent with his friends in West Lutton.

The mare clopped along, the man singing to keep them both company, when her ears suddenly pricked up. Music was being played somewhere to their right, towards the slopes of the Wolds. The farmer could just make out the black hump of Willey Howe, known for miles around as belonging to Themselves, the Good People, the Fairy Folk.

He had heard stories, of course; there was one about a fairy woman who, falling in love with a local man, used to leave him a daily piece of gold on top of the mound. The stupid man told a friend about it, causing his good luck to disappear along with his magical income. There were other stories too, all connected with treasure; the farmer had known them all his life and had scrambled all over the mound as a boy, looking for a way in, but he had long ceased to pay any attention to them. Now he drew rein while he and the mare listened to the unexpected music. It was not grand or mysterious, but merry; horns and sackbuts were playing a jolly dance. There was laughter too, and chatter – a party? Surely it couldn't be coming from that grim howe! Some band of travellers must be camped nearby.

Expecting to come upon a campfire any minute, he pushed his mare through the wet hawthorn scrub towards the mound which loomed huge against the hillside, hardly visible in the dim starlight. At first he saw nothing unusual, but then, as he began to circle the howe, he came upon a narrow stream of golden light pouring from a doorway in its side. The mare whickered nervously, but the farmer forced her closer. The sounds of laughter grew louder; now he could also hear the clinking of plates and glasses, the thump of dancing feet. Forgetting any danger in his curiosity, the farmer rode right up to the door and looked into the mound. It was much larger inside than out: a great hall lit by many flaming torches and candles. Beautifully dressed folk were dancing or feasting at tables covered with all sorts of unseasonable food. Though it was winter outside he saw strawberries, blackberries, new milk cheeses, spring lamb and kid. There were cowslips and primroses in golden bowls all around.

The farmer sat in the drizzle, staring in admiration and desire at the golden plates, goblets of finely carved glass, the shining white tablecloths and napkins. Even the knives had handles decorated with gold.

One of the many servants, who stood by, noticed the man outside and, filling one of the beautiful glass cups, came over and offered it to him.

'Come in and join us, traveller!' he said.

As the farmer raised the cup to his lips the old mare shook her mane and he suddenly came to his senses, realising his danger. Never take food or drink from the fairies or you will be theirs! Quickly – regretfully! – he poured the drink on to the ground – he wasn't about to give the cup back, though. The servant shouted as the mare leapt past him and carried the farmer swiftly off towards home.

Pursuit was not long in coming. First of all shouts followed him into the night, growing louder and more angry. Then he heard the sound of horses' hooves. He gripped the cup more tightly and bent low over the mare's neck. Water – water was the thing; if he could just cross water ...The Gypsey Race, a mere trickle in that time of peace, was not far away. With one last effort the mare splashed through it and then they were safe on the other side. The farmer looked over his shoulder as his pursuers milling around, baffled, on the other side of the river, unable to cross water. Finally, with many shouted insults, they rode away back to Willey Howe.

The famer kept the cup for some years as evidence of his adventure. He probably would have preferred a gold one, but glass was very rare at the time and this was a deep crimson,

beautifully and wonderfully carved with spring flowers. Several such fairy cups still exist and bring luck to the families that own them.

Later (foolishly, in my opinion) he gave it to his overlord, who in time gave it to King Henry I, who in turn gave it to David I, King of Scotland. No doubt it now lies in some royal treasury, its magical origin forgotten – if it hasn't been broken by a careless servant, that is.

THE SCREAMING SKULL

Burton Agnes

The Griffyth sisters were young and beautiful, born to consequence and wealth. They came of an ancient, respected family; their grandfather had been knighted by Henry VIII on the famous Field of the Cloth of Gold and their father, Sir Henry, had improved his fortune at the court of Queen Elizabeth. However, the days of castles were almost over and Sir Henry had decided to follow the fashion of the time by building for himself a new house, lighter and brighter than the old fortified manor house where he lived; somewhere where he could entertain his noble friends in a civilised, modern way.

His family took a keen interest in this grand project, none more so than his youngest daughter, christened Catherine but always known by her second name, Anne. She never tired of discussing matters such as the pros and cons of including a long gallery for wet weather exercise, or how best to support the newfangled great oaken staircase.

Such a house was an expensive long-term project, but as the family was determined not to knock down the old place (to sell the stone, as others might have done) they continued to live in it much as they had always done, while the new house of their dreams rose under its narrow windows.

The new manor house was to be built not of stone but of warm orange brick. Instead of the sober darkness of the old place there was to be light everywhere, light pouring in through long windows of expensive glass. Sir Henry had learnt long ago at court the importance of appearance. Such windows would announce to any travellers on the Bridlington road that the house's owner was a rich and powerful man.

Anne visited the house site frequently over the years of its building. As a little girl, she paced out the rooms; later she discussed its design with the architect, Robert Smythson, chief mason to Queen Elizabeth. For her, the house became as beloved and interesting as a member of the family.

Ten years went by; the house and the girls both grew up. As their new home neared completion excitement increased in the family. It was even more perfect than they had imagined, well-proportioned, beautiful, elegant. They hardly dared believe that they would soon be living there! The girls squabbled amiably over which bedrooms they would have. They imagined themselves sweeping gracefully down the new stairs, fans in their hands, rather than bunching their skirts up to teeter precariously down the manor's spiral staircases.

Perhaps great wealth attracts great jealousy: it certainly attracted greed. A motley gang of thieves, such as haunted the wilder parts of England in those days, learnt of the riches of the family. They must have laid their plans carefully. How else would they have known that Anne had been away on a visit to her friends the St Quintins at Harpham?

Early one evening the Griffyth coach, swaying and creaking, drawn by sweating horses, whipped on by a dishevelled coachman, came clattering into the yard. The servants ran out.

'For God's sake!' cried the coachman, 'Look to the young mistress – she's been stabbed!'

At that moment Anne, white as her smock, opened the carriage door and fell out on to the cobbles. Inside the coach her maid was screaming and crying. They carried Anne into the castle and laid her on the great table in the hall while the doctor and surgeon were sent for. They staunched the bloody knife wound in her side but shook their heads and looked grave. Who could tell what internal organs had been damaged?

The poor coachman, shaking and weeping, told a confused story. As the trip home to Burton Agnes was such a short one they had set out from the St Quintins' house without the outriders who usually accompanied them on journeys. A band of men – the coachman couldn't see how many in the darkness – had ambushed them not far from the village. They had leapt on the coach, held a dagger to his throat and forced Anne and her maidservant to get out.

'She were right brave, sirs, and asked them, did they not know who she were? But they cared not a rush for that but bid her remove her jewels; for, they said, with many an oath, they would have 'em and those of her maid too. I could not see what happened as I were up on the coach box, but I heard one man growl "and I'll have THAT too!" Whereupon my lady says, brave as you please, "That were given to me by my godmother, pray let me keep it." Then the man says, beggin' your ladies' pardon, "Deny me awt, thou filthy whore! That's for thee, then!" Well, Sirs, there came a scream and much shouting. The man holding me swore, then he jumped down and they was all away into the darkness with my poor mistress leaning against the coach, clasping her side and the maid in strong hysterics. I put 'em both into the coach. "Take me home, John," she says, "for I fear I am dying" and so I drives home as quick as I could.'

Sir Henry's men scoured the countryside for many days looking for the gang, but they had melted away, nor could anyone give him any information about them.

Anne's wound was deep, but it might not have been fatal if infection had not set in. Soon she was sinking beneath a burning fever. Her sisters watched at her bedside, praying. As the fever took hold, Anne began to hallucinate and talk wildly. The main thing her mind turned to was the house, still unfinished. 'I must see it! I belong to it! Take me there!'

Her sisters restrained her, but she wept and struggled weakly against them, muttering about plasterwork and paint. Then, just before she died, her eyes opened and she seemed to see her sisters clearly.

'My death is near,' she told them calmly. 'Listen to me, my dear sisters. I cannot be parted from the house. My heart is in it and I can't be separated from it. Promise me now that you will bury part of me in it – for if you do not I fear I shall never rest quietly in my grave.'

The sisters didn't know what to say. How could they deny her this last wish, and, yet, what would their father say to this strange unholy request? They promised, of course, soothed her, saw her relax, heard her last faint prayers, but after she had died and her burial was being organised, they had to tell their father what she had asked.

'Anne's mind was wandering towards the end. My daughter shall be buried whole, as befits her state, not hacked up like a side of beef. It is out of the question.'

And so Anne was buried in the old church, her sarcophagus resting beside those of her ancestors.

Shortly after the funeral the family said goodbye to the old manor and moved into the new house. It was not the joyful occasion they had all looked forward to for so long, and yet the serene beauty of the place comforted them in their grief.

Not for long.

They had barely enjoyed a week in the house before uncanny things began to happen; noises, mostly, thumps and bumps at first, then sudden screams and violent hand-clapping. The servants took to their heels and refused to come back.

The family was distraught; first Anne and now this! The sisters whispered together and went to see the vicar. They told him about Anne's last words.

'Our father talks of an exorcism for demons, but we believe that this trouble is caused by Anne's unsatisfied ghost.'

'Well, my children, it may be so, but do you realise that to fulfil your sister's wishes we would have to violate the sanctity of her tomb? That is a serious matter. Come now, don't look so unhappy, I shall speak to your father.'

By this time things at the house were getting so bad that, with the vicar's encouragement, Sir Henry at last agreed to the exhumation.

It was a sober group, father and daughters still dressed in mourning black, that stood in the Griffyth chapel, watching the stonemason remove the lead that sealed the stone covering

on Anne's sarcophagus. The vicar waited by nervously; he had known Anne since she was a baby – indeed he had baptised her – but the prospect of her vengeful ghost unnerved him.

Two strong servants took hold of the stone cover and slid it carefully aside. Inside was a fine wooden coffin. Tension grew as its fastenings too were removed. At last the lid was lifted. Everyone leant forward.

'Great God!' exclaimed Sir Henry.

One of the servants crossed himself (and then remembered that he wasn't supposed to do that anymore). The girls burst into tears and the vicar into prayer.

'Angels and ministers of grace defend us!'

Anne's body lay, completely uncorrupted, dressed in her funeral garments exactly as when she had been buried. Her hands, still holding a posy of flowers were clasped on her breast, but her head – her head was lying between her feet! The fine skin had rotted away, the bright hair fallen out and her teeth gleamed alarmingly in what was now just a skull. Anne's wishes were crystal clear.

They took the horrible thing back to the new house with them, wrapped tenderly in a piece of linen. A place of honour was prepared for it and soon, washed and waxed, it was presiding over the great hall. From the moment it entered the house all haunting ceased. The servants were eventually persuaded to return and the life of a great house slowly recommenced, blessed, it seemed, by its new presiding spirit.

Over the years, subsequent owners were not so willing to have a skull on permanent display, but each time it was removed from the house the hauntings recommenced. Even attempts to bury it decently in the churchyard failed. 'Awd Nance' as Anne's ghost was now known, raised hell until her skull was returned home. Eventually it was bricked into the house she loved so well. I know where it is, but I'm not telling you!

JEANNIE O' BIGGERSDALE

Lythe
Mulgrave Woods belong to the family of the Marquis of
Normanby who live in Mulgrave Castle, a fine eighteenth-
century house. However, this tale comes from a time before it
was built, when another family, the Radcliffes, lived in Foss
Castle, the remains of which now lie deep in Mulgrave Woods.
It was said to have been built by the giant, Wade (see North
Yorkshire Folk Tales*). Nearby a certain spirit known as*
Jeannie o' Biggersdale was popularly believed to live in a dark-
some cave.

In Lythe, a village at the top of the steep hill out of Sandsend,
they were firing the stiddy [a type of anvil] in honour of the
marriage of the lord of Foss Castle. The whole village was
there watching as the stiddy was ceremoniously carried out
and turned upside down. The hole in the base was filled
with gunpowder and the blacksmith stood by to fire it with a
red-hot iron when the happy couple came past.

It was not a particularly ancient tradition – though anvils
had always been regarded as a bit magic – but it was good fun
and made the lasses jump and squeal satisfyingly.

John Roe, a farmer's son, was there with his mates, keen for
a look at the new bride. As they waited they chatted, as usual,
about women.

'So, John, has Betty looked tha way yet?'

'Yes, John, has she stopped looking down that pretty nose yet?'

John sighed. 'It's not my fault if I have a good eye for a lass.
But she's already getten a follower, it seems. Jamie Pearson
is dangling at her tail as close as sheep shit. Seems I mun
look otherwhere.'

'Well, thoo'd better get on wi' it or all the lasses'll be taken.'

'Yes, and thoo'll be left wi' Jeannie o' Biggersdale!'

John was aware of his father's eye on him or he would have responded to his friend's teasing with mild physical violence. Instead he assumed a knowing air. 'Ah, but who's ever seen Jeannie o' Biggersdale? She's one of the Good Folk, isn't she? She might be a rare beauty just waiting for a strong lad to woo her!' The hoots of derision which greeted this utterance were silenced by calls of 'Shh! They're coming!'

The newly-weds, fresh from the church, flanked by servants and family, with sprigs of rosemary and ribbon favours tied to their arms, were advancing slowly along the village street. Before them went four maidens carrying huge pastry-covered wedding cakes – the weight was supported by silk scarves around the girls' necks. A page boy, proudly embarrassed, strode at the head of the procession, carrying a silver cup decorated with ribbons and gilded rosemary.

The procession stopped in front of the smithy and the young groom spoke to the smith in a friendly manner, bidding him, 'Do your office!' The smith took the red-hot iron from the fire and applied it to the powder-loaded anvil. There was a hiss, a flash and a tremendous bang that made one of the bridesmaids nearly drop her cake. A babble of laughter and jokes followed; the young couple (the bride with her hands still pressed over her ears) moved on, leaving an invitation for all to come to the castle for beer and cake.

John and his friends followed and were soon drinking deep of the bridal ale, barrels of which were set out in the castle courtyard.

'Now,' said Ned, surfacing with beery foam on his nose and pointing at the bride, 'THERE's a real rare beauty!'

'But that sort are not for us, boys!' replied Robin.

'That's just blether!' The ale was stronger than any of them was used to; John was already a little belligerent. 'Not all beauties are noble born. Why shouldn't we find 'em?'

'Well, there's none round here,' laughed Robin, casting a critical eye over the village maidens. 'Not free, any rate. No, tha'd better settle for Jeannie!'

John's mind had been vaguely running on Jeannie o' Biggersdale as he and his friends had walked to the castle and he immediately took up the subject. 'Why has no one ever seen her? How do we know that there IS a Jeannie? Happen she's just an old dame's tale.' His friends exchanged glances. 'Come on, John, everyone knows she exists! Why else would people be afraid to go into the woods? Who fritted the wits out of young Harry? I don't know what kind she belongs to but all agree she'll do damage if tha interferes wi'her.'

John snorted. 'Likely she's just some bugaboo to frit bairns!'

'Well,' retorted Ned, somewhat nettled, 'I'll wager thoo wouldn't dare go looking for her!'

John fired up immediately. 'I'll take thy wager. How much?' Robin, worried, tried to change the subject, but it was no good; John had the bit between his teeth now and he was, as they said 'stunt [stubborn] as a mule'; besides, didn't he stand to win some easy money? He made his wager with Ned.

Thinking about it next morning – with a thumping headache to boot – it didn't seem such a good idea, but John wasn't one to back down. He had work to do for his father during the next few days, but as soon as he had a free afternoon he saddled up his pony and rode off to Mulgrave Woods to take up Ned's dare. Naturally he didn't tell his family where he was going.

As he rode he thought about Jeannie. His granny, who knew a thing or two, had always said that if Jeannie was left alone the land would flourish. 'She's a thing left over mebbe from old times or one of Themselves [fairies].' She was supposed to live in Hob Cave, wherever that was. As a lad he and his friends had looked for it, playing heroes, but never too far from the safety of Lythe. Now, though, he was a fearless adult with a tough little fell pony. He trotted down the track past Foss Castle and on into the woods. At first the trees were spread apart where the undergrowth had been cleared close to the castle. Further along, though, the woods drew in dark and threatening, where little becks cut deep channels overhung with bushes. Soon John was in thick woodland where progress over the broken land was hard. Now he was leading the pony, following a dry ditch downwards, slashing at brambles with his dagger. He hoped that the cave would be at the bottom. At the back of his mind was the uncomfortable thought that he really should have made a plan.

Then the pony raised his head and John caught the smell of smoke ahead. He slipped the pony's reins over a branch and crept forwards. He pushed through a big tangle of ivy and there it was in front of him: Hob Cave, a black hole in the sandstone cliff. A small fire was burning in front of it and there were a few pots lying about. Until that very moment John had still been playing heroes; he had not quite believed in his heart of hearts that there really was a Jeannie. Now he did, but the very ordinariness of the grubby pots told against her being a fairy. Perhaps she was an ordinary woman – with a spell on her, perhaps? An evil stepmother? He, John, could rescue her! In an instant the scenario unfolded before him: the beautiful grateful woman, the happy father reunited with his daughter; the riches showered on her saviour. John stood tall and moved forward to the mouth of the cave.

'Jeannie?' he called. 'Jeannie o' Biggersdale?' He heard someone moving about in the darkness. 'Don't be afraid! I won't hurt–' He got no further, for out of the cave, shrieking like a banshee, came a horrible figure, arms like winter branches reaching out for him. It might have once been a woman, but its contorted face, pointed teeth, matted hair and red eyes left no doubt in John's mind that flight was his only option. He ran for the pony, stumbling on bramble whips that seemed to writhe about him. He leapt on to the terrified pony's back and hung on for dear life as it broke into a gallop. The ground was treacherous. They swerved between trees, sprung over fallen timber, leaped ditches. When John glanced over his shoulder it seemed that they had thrown off their pursuer. Panting as hard as the pony, John reined it back to a walk. The sun was going down; darkness seemed to rise up all around them like the tide creeping up the beach.

For a few steps John thought all was well. Then, with a hideous tearing snarl, Jeannie burst out of the bushes right in front of him. Both he and the horse cried out and fled, dark stripes of blood welling up from shoulder and flank where her claws had raked them

'Water!' John shouted to himself. 'Cross water Granny said! Fairies can't cross water! Where's water?' Mickleby Beck – that was somewhere around here – or East Row Beck. Desperately he turned the pony's head this way and that as he looked for the dip that would indicate a stream.

Jeannie, shriek and howl though she might, had not been able to keep up with them, but he could hear her crashing about not very far behind. All at once a steep bank opened in front of him. In the growing darkness he thought he could catch a glitter of water. John urged the tired pony towards it. It flowed in a small cleft, too awkward for the pony to manage. They would have to jump. John peered forward to judge the distance; he thought it was possible.

'Come on, lad, you can do it!'

The pony gathered itself, but Jeannie was closer than John had reckoned. She sprang out of a bush of broom behind them and as the pony leapt she struck a blow on its rump with her hideous branch-like arm. The pony reached the other side, its hooves scrabbling on the crumbling bank. Then it seemed to stumble awkwardly, throwing John off. Winded, he rolled, gasped, scrambled to his feet. His hands and his clothes were suddenly dripping with a hot dark liquid, was it blood? On the other bank of the beck, Jeannie shook her withered fists at him, then turned and disappeared into the night. John looked down at the pony, groaning and thrashing about at his feet. One glance was enough to send him running, howling like a baby: Jeannie's blow had cut it in half.

THE DRUMMING WELL

Harpham

Lord St Quintin was sick, sick to death, they said, and yet he refused to make a will or to receive the last rites of the Church. He sat propped in his great bed in his manor house in Harpham, reading the more titillating columns of the *York Courant*, and it seemed that he laughed at death.

Scandalised by this careless behaviour, his son, returned from his Oxford college to be near his father in his illness, begged him to think of his immortal soul.

'Fiddlesticks!' said his father, 'I'm not going to die yet. Go and get your dinner!'

The son, deeply upset, confided in his old nurse. 'It's as if he thinks that death can't take him,' he said, almost in tears.

'Ah!' said she. 'That's because he hasn't heard the drumming yet.'

The boy stared at her. 'What drumming?'

She laughed. 'Oh, Master Phillip, have you forgotten the old tale after all this time? Or – wait a minute – have you still not heard it? I wanted to tell it to you when you were a lad but your lady mother forbade me. Pagan superstition, she held it to be. Have you really still not heard of the curse of the St Quintins?'

The boy shook his head in confusion. 'We're under a curse?'

'Well, it's not exactly a curse – just a sort of warning. You know the Drumming Well?'

He nodded; it was not far from the back of the manor itself. 'Of course I do! What of it?'

'Did you never question why it was called that?'

'I was told that some drummer boy had drowned in it, that's all.'

'That's true, but it was a St Quintin that put him there. Well, your lady mother is long dead now and you will soon be head of the family unless God does indeed spare your father. It's time you heard the full story.

'Hmm! Where to start? You know that every Englishman is supposed to prepare for war by practising his bowmanship at the butts?'

'I'm not an infant, Nurse, of course I know – used to shoot once, myself – but I don't know anyone in Oxford who respects that old law now; guns are much more use in war!'

'Guns! Nasty violent things. Blow your head off if you're not careful!'

'Get on with the tale, Nurse.'

'Well, in the days when every man in the village used to practise there was a lot of competition, specially between the young men. So, one of your ancestors – I can't remember his name – organised a feast day to be held once a year when the best archers could compete together for prizes – a side of bacon or a barrel of beer or suchlike.

'Now, there was at that time a woman in the village reputed a witch, though it seems no one could ever prove it. Molly Hewson, her name was, and she had a son, Tom, who was held to be the finest archer of the lot. He was a strapping lad who also played the drum in the village waits band. He was such a good archer that your ancestor had appointed him as trainer of the village archers.

'On one of these feast days the men were gathered all together to shoot at the butts – they were nearer to the Drumming Well in those days. Now on this day there was a great press of folk, villagers and gentry both, and your ancestor as well, keen to show off to his friends the skill of his own village men. Tom was there, of course, playing to enliven the event with the other musicians. He was beating his drum and waiting for his turn to shoot. Being the best archer, you see, he got to shoot last.

'I expect you'll remember from your own archery days that a clean loose is one of the most essential skills of shooting?'

'Yes, if you don't let the arrow go quickly enough it drops short.'

'Well, your ancestor was particularly proud of how cleanly all the village men loosed their arrows, but on this day there was one fellow who kept plucking his bowstring like a harp. Lord St Quintin watched him shoot a couple of arrows and then he could bear it no longer and rushed to correct him. Unfortunately there was a big crowd, as I said, and as he strode forwards he bumped into Tom Hewson and knocked him and his drum into the well.'

'Lord save us!'

'They tried to get him out, of course; threw him a rope and so on, but it was a deep well, and by the time they had lowered someone down to him he had drowned.

'Well, they brought him up and laid him on the grass. They wrapped him up in blankets and warmed him by the blacksmith's fire, hoping that he would come to life again, as has been known. The priest said lots of prayers, but it became obvious that his spirit had gone for good.

'His mother was told and she came running, tearing her hair and wailing. She threw herself on his body – you can imagine the scene. No doubt people would have been kind to her, even though she was feared as a witch, but suddenly she ups and points her skinny finger at St Quintin.

'"You killed my son!" she screams, spit flying everywhere. It was no use telling her that it was an accident; she didn't care. All she knew was that her son was dead and that a St Quintin was responsible.

'"May you and all St Quintins be cursed!" she cried. "From now on whenever one of you is going to die my poor dead son will beat his drum for very joy!"

'The people around her thought she just spoke wildly in her grief, but shortly before your ancestor died the sound of a drum was heard. It came from the well!

'And so it is, Master Philip, from that day to this. The drum warns of a St Quintin's death.'

'Have you ever heard it yourself, Nurse?'

'No, for I was far from home when your grandfather died. There has been no noise of it recently and that is why your poor father still has hopes for his recovery.'

That very evening, as the son sat at table with the old nurse, there came a profound low sound that reverberated throughout the old house: the beating of a drum deep in the earth. Louder and louder it grew, shaking the walls and setting the pigeons on the roof flying. The old nurse clutched her heart and the son leapt to his feet, glancing wildly around. He ran to his father's bedroom, but it was no use: the old man was dead!

6

VILLAINY

The Babe in the Wood

Beverley

A hunting gentleman living near Beverley is having a bad night's sleep. He tosses and turns, muttering. His long-suffering wife finally wakes him.

'Whatever is the matter, William? Are you having a bad dream?'

He looks around, confused. 'No, not a bad dream, dearest, but a perplexing one. I dreamed that someone was talking to me urgently, telling me that I should get up and look for something, something unexpected.'

'Perhaps it is a bad omen. Perhaps you should not go hunting today?'

'What? Because of a dream? How my friends would laugh!'

And so he dresses in the dark of a winter's morning and goes off to his hunt.

As hounds stream away after a fox across Beverley Westwood, our gentleman is having trouble with his new hunter, which is young and inexperienced. Soon they are quite far behind. As they canter through a wood the horse shies so violently that he is nearly thrown. He looks around to see what has alarmed it and catches a movement in the trees.

Instantly his dream comes into his mind. He dismounts and tries to lead his horse towards the place, but it is being silly, rolling its eyes and pulling away. He loops the reins over a branch. There is the movement again! High up in a mossy tree. He advances quietly, craning his neck. There is a big hole in the side of the tree; he peers in and gasps ... Inside, very dirty, cold and miserable, there is a small girl, hardly more than a baby. A filthy cloth is tied tightly around her mouth so she can only make a little moaning noise. When she sees him, she freezes in terror, but he speaks kindly to her and eventually she lets him reach in and pick her up. She is soiled, smelly and very weak, though she clings to him in a way that touches his heart as he remounts his horse and rides slowly home, hunting forgotten.

His wife exclaims with horror at his story, but she knows what to do and soon the little girl is washed, fed a little gruel – 'Not too much on a starving stomach' – and put into a warm bed.

'Whoever put her in there stopped her mouth to prevent her crying,' the outraged wife tells our gentleman, 'they must have wanted her dead; she's as thin as a lath and as cold as a paddock [toad]. If you had not found her she would have died by morning – she may die even yet.'

It is touch and go for many days, but the little girl does not die. The hunting gentleman and his wife make many enquiries locally to try to find her parents, but no one admits to having lost a little girl, so they continue to look after her. She is only about two and does not seem able to speak, though the shock of her experience may have robbed her of what words she has. As the weeks go by, however, she puts on weight and begins to respond to her new parents.

'God has not blessed us with our own children, but His Providence has sent us this baby as a comfort,' says the gentleman to his wife. 'Let us get her a proper nurse.'

Christmas approaches. On the Eve the house is decked
with the usual ivy and holly. The little girl toddles around,
holding tightly to her nurse's hand, but looking at everything
with interest.

'Oh! Listen, William,' says the wife, 'isn't that music outside? The Singing Women have come. We must let them in.'

The Singing Women travel the neighbourhood at Christmas, earning pennies and gifts of food from the more well-off. When they have sung some carols and been rewarded with a big bag of nuts and apples as well as some money, one of them spies the little girl.

'Is yon maid thy child, madam?' she asks. 'I though tha had none. Come hither, pretty!' She draws near to the child, who hides her face in her nurse's skirt. 'Would'st like an apple?' The little girl turns to look, but the Singing Woman backs away, her eyes wide.

'Well I niver!' she gasps. 'She's the dead spit of Mary Somes!' The other Singing Women gather round. 'Look! She's the dead spit of poor little Mary Somes what 'as bin dead and buried this last month!'

The hunting gentleman has, of course, heard of Squire Somes of Beverley; the world of county gentry is small. The squire himself has been dead for six months or so, reputedly of grief after his wife's death. The gentleman makes inquiries of his friends. Did Squire Somes ever have a daughter called Mary? Yes, they say, and entrusted her on his deathbed to his brother, Thomas. She would have inherited a large part of her father's estate when she came of age, but, alas, the poor little thing died a month ago. The hunting gentleman suggests that this was extremely convenient for the uncle, who would now get the whole estate, but his friends pooh-pooh his suspicions. 'Oh no, her death was all quite above board,' they tell him. 'No expense spared on the funeral. The coffin was open so that everyone could see that there had been no foul play.'

The hunting gentleman is not so easily put off. He discusses the matter with the local magistrate. 'Well,' says the magistrate, scratching thoughtfully under his wig, 'it could be nothing more than coincidence. One baby looks pretty much like another to me. Still, there may be something in it. Never much cared for Thomas myself. Something shifty about the eyes. Let's speak to the coroner about an exhumation.'

They dig up the little white coffin, much to the disgust of the locals who believe that the poor wee mite should be left in peace. Their disgust turns to anger, however, when in the coffin is found, not the body of a baby, but a wax dummy.

Thomas Somes is speedily arrested and brought to trial at the next assize. As Mary is still alive, he can only be tried for attempted murder, but to that charge is added one of causing solemn rites to be held for a false burial. Once in court, Thomas acts the injured party. Some neighbour, he asserts, stole the child – though who and for what reason is unclear – and being afraid that suspicion of killing the dear little thing (to whom, he assures the court, he has always behaved with the tenderest care) would fall upon him, he organised the false funeral at considerable cost to himself. He knew that the Church might condemn him, but he was certain that God would not be offended, especially as he had always loved Mary and been devastated by her loss.

It is just possible that this ingenious argument might have swayed the court in Thomas' favour were it not for the witnesses' testimony against him.

The first says that although he had been told by Mr Somes that the child was dying, he had, with his own eyes, seen her playing, apparently in perfect health.

The second, a maid, says, with East Riding frankness, that from the moment Mr Somes brought the child home he 'grudged it every bit and drop it had' and, furthermore, 'was so cross to it that it trembled at the very sight of him!'

Most damning of all is the third witness, a poor tenant of Mr Somes.

'He took me to t'Sun [a local pub] and said that he were right pleased wi'me as a tenant and that I might live rent free if I would do summat for him. I were suspicious, naturally enough, and said, what were it he wanted me to do? He leant over very confidential-like and said it were nobbut making away wi'his niece, Mary. I didn't grasp his meaning at first, but then he said it again, and that the poor lamb was so sickly that it would be doing it a kindness to kill it.'

Mr Somes turns to the witness with a face of fury, but the judge quells him with a look.

'And did you agree to do this heinous crime?'

'Certainly not, yer honour. I'm not so sackless [foolish], tha knows. I refused him straight out – though I knew it would not end well for me.'

'And how did Mr Somes take your refusal?'

'Well, my Lord, he went as black as thunner and threated some, but seein' that I held my ground he left the inn with a right monk on.'

'I beg your pardon?'

'In a rage, my Lord.' (That's the clerk.)

The trial is done. The verdict: Guilty! Only the sentence remains. The judge looks solemn.

'This is an unusual crime, gentlemen; unusual, and so evil that I intend to make an example of Thomas Somes to warn all relatives against committing such crimes. If it wasn't for this gentleman' – a nod towards the hunting gentleman – 'this would be a murder trial. Somes' intention to kill Mary is clear, though he did not have the courage to do the deed himself but hoped that cruel starvation and deprivation would do it for him. My sentence is this. First, that Thomas Somes, gent., should stand fined 800 marks. Secondly, that he should remain in prison until the money is paid. Thirdly, that he should suffer two years' imprisonment if he does not pay the fine. Lastly, that he shall stand three market days in the pillory, once in Beverley, once in his own town and once in York City. Finally, I entrust Mary to the guardianship of the gentleman who rescued her and who will, we understand, find great pleasure providing suitably for her future and education.'

The sentence is not as lenient as it might seem to us: the pillory will probably lead to serious physical damage being inflicted on Mr Somes by a public particularly incensed at his dastardly crime – a broken nose, almost certainly, and possibly permanent damage to his eyes or ears.

As for Mary, she knows nothing of her wicked uncle's fate, playing happily with her new family, secure in the hunting gentleman's house.

The Penny Hedge

Whitby

Long ago the Forest of Eskdale belonged to the abbey of St Hilda at Whitby. It was wide and deep and filled with deer and boar. Local lords loved to hunt there, specially on fine autumn mornings when the air was cold and sweet and the leaves golden.

There was a monk at the abbey who longed for more solitude. He had grown weary of the trivialities of the monastery; the sleepy shuffling and yawning at the early service, the surreptitious gossiping in the refectory, the small jealousies and petty spites of men shut up with each other for years. He longed for a more austere life. He pestered the authorities until at last they gave him permission to live as a hermit in the forest.

He built a small hermitage for himself, part chapel, part monk's cell, and began his solitary life. The forest animals soon got used to his silent figure sitting in the doorway or walking slowly among the trees as he gathered firewood. He himself became familiar with the life of the forest, in its own way as busy as any monastery. Birds came for his scraps; foxes sniffed at the door; great striped badgers rolled past in the evening hunting for worms and beetles in the underbrush. Sometimes deer would watch him for a while and then fade away into the leaves without a sound.

One morning, in golden October weather, three young lords, William de Bruce, Ralph de Percy and their friend Allatson of Fylingdales, came hunting boar in Eskdale forest with horns and hounds. The hermit could hear the horns and the huntsmen shouting and striking the bushes to rouse the boar. He went into his hermitage to pray.

The huntsmen soon roused a big old boar and pursued him hotly, cheering on their boarhounds with whoops. The chase was long and the whole forest rang with the noise. Eventually one of the young lords managed to wound their quarry and it began to tire. Soon it was looking for a place to hide or to turn at bay. It came to the hermit's chapel and the open door and the darkness inside looked like safety. The boar rushed in.

A wounded boar is not a thing to face weaponless. The hermit had nothing but his faith so he remained silent and watched the beast. It coughed and sank to its knees right in front of the altar as if it were praying. The sound of the horns and the baying of the hounds was close now. The boar turned towards the hermit and its dimming eyes begged for help. In a moment the hermit had shut the door and stood with his back against it.

He heard the hounds burst into his clearing and the sound of hooves. He didn't know whether boars had souls or not but he began to pray for it anyway. The dogs began to leap and scratch at the door with their nails. Booted feet approached. A loud banging came at the door. The hermit kept praying.

The banging redoubled. 'Hermit! Open this door!' The boar
lay panting on its side; it was dying.

'Do not disturb a monk at his prayers!' the hermit shouted back.

'Open this door or by God we'll kick it down!'

The hermit knelt by the boar's head.

Crashing and shouting. The door was broken with a hastily snatched-up log. Sudden light and then darkness as three big men entered the hermitage. The hermit was flung aside like a leaf.

'God's bones! The brute's died on us!' growled one of the men, bending down to look at the boar. 'We've missed the kill!' he kicked the lifeless body. 'I swear by my sword, old man, you're going to pay for this!'

When they left the hermitage carrying the boar, the hermit lay motionless in its place, bleeding from many wounds. How he was found, whether it was by the lad who brought his daily food or by the abbot himself is uncertain, but the story tells that he lived long enough to be carried to the monastery. There he told his story and named his attackers.

As soon as they knew that the hermit lived the three lords went on the run to Scarborough, where they took sanctuary in the church. They were noblemen's sons so they thought that they would soon be pardoned. Unfortunately for them the abbot of St Hilda's abbey was a friend of the king and he gave orders that they be taken up as common criminals. The hermit, who lay quietly in the infirmarium, growing weaker every day, heard that his injurers were to be con-demned to death. With his last strength he begged the abbot to hear him. 'I freely forgive those young men. They should not die.'

The abbot objected, saying that the king wished them to be punished for wounding a monk.

'It is not right for the Church to seek the death penalty. My life is leaving me. Let them go free, but let them do penance instead. This is my last request.'

The abbot could not deny the dying man, but he was determined to impose an exceptional penance on the young lords:

William de Bruce, Ralph de Percy, Allatson of Fylingdales, this is my doom on you:

Each Ascension Eve you will go to Stray Head Wood at sunrise and there each will receive from my Abbot officer ten stakes, ten stout stowers and ten yedders, each cut with a penny knife. You will carry these on your backs to the river bank at Stray Head End by Littlebeck and there on Ascension Day before nine in the morning you will each build a hedge or fence at the edge of the low tide. Each stake shall be a yard from the next and you shall so yedder them with yedders and stake them on each side with stout stowers that they can stand for three tides without being washed away. And the better to call your evil deed to remembrance a man shall sound a horn and another cry out 'Out on ye! Out on ye! Out on ye!' If you or your successors shall fail thus to build a hedge that shall withstand three tides, then the lands they now hold shall be forfeit to the Abbot of Whitby.

The descendants of the three lords have long since died out, but the Horngarth (or Penny Hedge) has continued to be built every year from that day to this.

Afterword

One day when I was in Whitby I noticed a miserable set of little sticks poking out of the mud of the harbour. I realised with some disappointment that this was the remains of that year's Horngarth. 'Stout' it was not!

Unfortunately, history does not really correspond at this story – although a building still referred to as the Hermitage, a rather sturdy stone chapel, still exists, behind Manor Farm. The three men had no equivalent in real life although their families did exist and the Allatsons were still responsible for building the Horngarth until their estate was sold in the eighteenth century.

The Milking Stool

Ugthorpe

Time out of mind witches have stolen milk from cows. If your prize milker suddenly goes dry or fails to give as much milk as before, don't go for the vet: look for the witch.

They have magic ways of transporting the stolen milk to wherever they want it; not for them the telltale bucket. Take the milch cows of Ugthorpe near Scarborough, for example. When one of them went dry the farmer shook his head; when two went dry, he ground his teeth and muttered about witches; when three went dry he walked up the street and stood hesitating outside a little cottage. Then he went home. When four went dry he threw his hat on the ground in fury, jumped on it and stumped off to get the neighbours. 'Where's tha gannin'?' his wife shouted after him.

'To have it out with Ann Allan, t'awd witch!'

'Mind her evil eye!'

The group of men walked nervously up the street to Ann's cottage. The farmer banged on her door. After a lot of muttered oaths and delay, Ann opened it and her puffy malevolent face looked out.

'Aye?' she said. 'Good day Farmer Cole and what brings thoo to my door? Lost summut?' She looked around at the neighbours. 'And I see tha's bringed company to fritten a poor awd woman!' she sneered.

'Thoo's bin stealing my milk, tha wicked old hag!'

Ann's face was a picture of outraged innocence.

'Who, ME? Vile lies! I should tak thoo ter law for libel!'

'I've seen thoo starin' an' starin' at them coos, twice, thrice a day.'

'So a poor awd body can't even take a walk and look on the land now-a-days. What are we comin' too?' she retorted.

'Why tha foul, stinkin'—'

The farmer was so angry and frustrated by this that, having exhausted his few arguments, he picked up a three-legged stool that stood by the door. He was about to heave it at Ann's head when he felt his hand getting wet. Something liquid was running down his sleeve. He stared at the stool in amazement. All the neighbours, who had been standing well back in case they were hurt by Ann's well-known evil eye, now crowded around.

From the legs of the stool poured streams of white creamy fresh milk.

'Tha's gitten it!' esclaimed one old man. 'That's what she steals t'milk in!'

'Aye,' said another, 'no wonder her fuzzocks [pigs] have grown so fat. She's bin feeding 'em thy milk!'

Exactly how the stool worked is never explained, but with this undeniable evidence of her wickedness, Ann was sentenced to the punishment of being made to walk in her chemise three times through the town. She was in full view of all her neighbours who made sure that she had a 'good taste of t'other end of coo' before she had finished.

PEGGY FLAUNDERS

Well known for a witch as Ann was, she was nothing to Peggy Flaunders, who lived right up in the north of the county, at Upleatham near Marske-on-Sea. She was a real person, living on well into the 1800s, and must have been a striking figure in her red cloak and tall hat. Various tales are told of her, good as well as bad, for if she liked you, you prospered.

For some reason Peggy Flaunders took against Tom Pearson; as a result all his cattle died and so, no longer able to afford to renew the tenancy of his farm, he passed it on to his cousin Bob. Now Bob quite liked Peggy with her gruff ways and sly humour. He had once done her a favour, but he only realised that he had also done himself one on the day he moved into the farm.

He had unlocked the door and was just lifting his foot to cross the threshold for the first time when his eye was caught by a flash of red in the lane. There stood Peggy, smiling for once. He nodded to her and as he entered the house he heard her call out 'Thoo has my good wishes!' Then, as his wife who was still standing outside, told him later, Peggy spun round three times, threw her red cloak on the ground, jumped over it, muttered some unintelligible words and walked away.

At first Bob's neighbours all foretold trouble. 'Ah, your beasts'll likely dwine and dwindle away like your cousin's,' said one, Hannah Rothwell.

'If a witch tells you summat good, likely it'll mean the opposite,' said another, Mary Parker. But apparently it didn't. Bob and his farm prospered; his cattle never fell ill or failed to give good milk – unlike those of Hannah and Mary.

Now, it seems that Peggy must have had some sort of a grudge against both women – or perhaps her pigs needed lots of feeding – because their cows refused to give good milk. Hannah couldn't get her butter to come. She churned the milk for hours with no result but a few floating white specks of butter and a whole lot of grey whey. Mary, on the other hand, had no trouble with churning – but that was because her cow gave so little milk that it was pointless putting it in the churn.

This state of affairs went on for several weeks with the women growing increasingly angry and worried. Eventually they were advised to consult a wise man, Johnathan Westcott, who lived at Upleatham. He was well known as a healer and spell-breaker.

Johnathan knew how to impress his female clients. (He was a tall well-looking man with a fine beard.) He treated them with grave respect while subtly implying that they were simple ignorant country women who had better leave everything to him.

When they had told him their problems he remained silent (his middle finger pressed to his forehead, his eyes closed) for so long that they began to think that he had gone to sleep. Then he suddenly shook himself (Mary, who was the nervous type, gave a little scream) and, fixing the two with burning eyes, he told them what they must do.

Hannah's churn, he said, was bewitched. She had to scald it out three times, first with boiling water and salt; next with boiling water with wicken [rowen] berries in it and thirdly with boiling water alone. Then she must drive a small wicken-wood peg into each end of the churn.

'And when next you churn you must say the following charm, looking into the churn as though looking for butter–'

'But there isn't any butter!'

'Yes, I know that, missus, but you must pretend you are looking – do you see? Look into the churn and say:

This time it's thine
Next time it's mine
Then mine for evermore!

Repeat this – have you memorised it? – repeat this, I say, nine times, turning the handle of the churn nine times between every repetition – would you like me to write it down? You can read, can't you …?'

For Mary's problem Mr Westcott had a different cure. He first consulted his almanac with some ceremony, staring at it, muttering and shaking his head. Then he told Mary that, starting on such and such a day, she should give the cow a drench and then not milk her fully for nine days. On the tenth day she should milk her properly, first whispering in her ear 'I'm milking thee for Peggy Flaunders.' If after that the cow didn't give proper amounts of milk then Peggy was not the witch responsible.

'If that is the case then you must find another suspect – or,' he added in an undertone, '– get rid of the cow.'

The two women did as he advised and, presumably (the sources don't tell us any more), Peggy's evil spells were foiled.

THE HAND OF GLORY

Whitby

I stare at the horribly shrivelled thing before me. It is a yellowish object, bones clearly visible, resembling a dried monkey's paw. I am in Whitby Museum (a gem of a place) and the thing is, the label tells me, a Hand of Glory. Excitement replaces disgust. This object was once regarded as the last word in technology for any aspiring robber or conspirator. It is a human hand cut, by tradition, from a hanged person. Dried, treated with spells, it was supposed to be able to burn like a candle. No one asleep in a house where it burned would be able to wake and any treasure there would be revealed.

Was it ever possible for those fingers to burn? Whose hand was it? Was it ever used? The label tells me no more.

The best-known version of this story is set at the Spital Inn on Bowes Moor, but there are others and because it's only in Whitby that you're ever likely to see a real Hand of Glory I am going to tell it here.

The big old inn stood in the middle of the desolate moor. It catered for the passing coach trade, providing stables, hot food, drink and beds for those who needed to sleep while their tired horses rested.

Late one windy rainy night there was a rapping at the door. The servant, Kitty, opened it but at first she could see no one for it was as dark as the pit of Hell outside, and her lantern shed little light on the new guest. Screwing up her eyes against the rain, Kitty saw a woman, well bundled up against the cold, bent over and dripping wet. Soft-hearted Kitty immediately felt sorry for her and hastened to bring her inside by the fire.

'I've got to leave very early in the morning,' murmured the woman, her voice husky. 'Please just let me sit here in the inglenook until dawn. I don't want to disturb anyone.'

When Kitty asked the landlord about the woman's request he was not pleased; the woman looked too poor to pay for anything. Poor guests had been known to steal the silver. He grumbled, though he couldn't very well turn her out into the rain, so he told Kitty that the unwelcome woman might sleep by the taproom fire, but that she, Kitty, must sleep on the settle in the same room to keep an eye on her.

The landlord and his family went to bed; the woman huddled in the warm inglenook and seemed to fall asleep. Kitty lay down on the long, hard, wooden settle to do the same. She looked at the guest through half-closed eyes, wondering who she was and why she was wandering the moor in the middle of the night. Her feet must be so sore, poor creature ... though, thought Kitty, suddenly curious ... she's wearing men's boots – HUGE men's boots. She peered through her lids at the woman's face, now more visible in the glow of the fire and then her blood seemed to freeze in her veins: the firelight illuminated a cruel mouth and a bristly chin: the guest was a man!

Kitty's heart raced and it was all she could do not to move. What should she do? He seemed quite bent and old and she was a strong lass, but she was not going to risk his being much fitter than he looked. Her best course was to pretend to be asleep and see what he got up to. Scared though she was, she closed her eyes, breathed more deeply and began gently snoring.

After a while she heard the traveller stir and get up. Kitty opened her eyes a tiny crack. He had pulled up his skirt, under which he was wearing trousers, and was rummaging around in his pockets. Then he held up to the light something that Kitty didn't recognise immediately. It looked like a dried and wizened monkey's paw. Ah, yes, now she knew what it was, from her granny's tales: a Hand of Glory! In her surprise she forgot to snore. The man swung around immediately, glancing at her, so, terrified, she gave a grunt or two and began to snore again.

The traveller watched her for what seemed an age, but eventually he decided that she really was asleep. He took a bottle out of his other pocket and poured a little liquid over the spikey fingers of the Hand of Glory. Then he took a wooden spill from the pot on the mantelpiece, lit it at the fire and proceeded to hold it to each of the fingers in turn. They caught

fire, burning with a cold blue flame and a nasty smell. Then the man came close to Kitty and, waving the flaming Hand before her face, said these words:

> Let those who rest more deeply sleep,
> Let those awake their vigils keep.
> O Hand of Glory shed thy light
> Direct us to our spoil tonight!

After that he fixed the Hand upright on the table and went to the outer door. Kitty heard him open it and whistle, three soft notes, several times repeated.

Kitty lifted her head. When she saw that the robber (for that was what he obviously was) had left the house, she jumped up and ran to the door. He was standing just outside on the top step so she crept up behind him and gave him a great push. He overbalanced and fell down the steps, giving her time to slam the door shut. She had a few minutes grace, fumbling desperately with the bolts, before he had picked himself up and was beating on the stout oak. Now Kitty could hear voices from what she supposed was the rest of the robber band. Would the door hold? What if they broke down one of the shutters and got in through a window?

She ran upstairs to her master's bedroom to wake him, but neither he nor his wife so much as stirred, though she shook and shouted at them. It was the same with the master's son and the other servants on the floor above; nothing would waken them.

For a moment Kitty stood at the top of the stairs, close to tears. Why wouldn't they wake? Then she cursed herself for a fool; of course they wouldn't wake! The Hand of Glory was still burning.

Quickly she ran downstairs. She didn't like to touch the thing, but she leant forward over it and blew on the flaming fingers. The flames bent and died for a second, then flamed up as brightly as ever. Screwing up her courage, she wet her own fingers and tried to pinch out them out, but still the baleful blue flames reignited.

Then from somewhere deep in her memory a piece of her Granny's folklore floated up. Milk! The purity of milk overcomes evil. Swiftly she ran down to the larder and fetched a jug of skimmed milk.

The banging was louder now, accompanied by the sound of cracking wood as one of the robbers tried to prise open a shutter. The fingers fizzled and spat as Kitty threw the milk over the Hand, but at last their flames were quenched.

Almost immediately she heard the folk above stirring. The landlord and his son came crashing downstairs, their clothes huddled on all anyhow. Kitty had no need to explain the situation. In a second the son had the shotgun down off the wall and was loading it. The landlord went to the door. He shouted for silence at the top of his powerful voice. Outside the robbers fell silent as they realised their plan had failed. (Kitty could hear them muttering to each other.) Then one shouted back 'All right, master, tha's won. Just give us back the Hand and we'll be gone!'

The landlord did not immediately reply. Instead he raised his eyebrows questioningly at his son, saw him nod, and silently drew back the bolts.

'This is all you'll get tonight!' he shouted as he flung the door wide. The son ran forward and fired. There was a howl of pain; the door was slammed again and locked.

They heard no more of the robbers after that, but in the morning they found splashes of blood outside and followed a bloody trail for quite a way up the road before they gave up. They never found the robbers and the men never returned for their Hand of Glory. What became of it? Who knows?

Perhaps someone gave it to the Whitby Museum ...

CRUEL PEG FYFE

Holderness

You might see her in a public house in Hedon or Patrington, a big, dark, flashy woman with a taste for bright colours and lots of gold rings. She'll be dominating the conversation, smoking her pipe or downing her quart with a group of rough men. Do you wonder at the meek silence of the locals? Are you surprised that a woman is allowed such freedom? Keep your thoughts to yourself, for this is Cruel Peg Fyfe, the terror of Holderness!

How Peg comes to be the leader of her brutal band of thugs is a mystery, but she knows that protection rackets can be as lucrative in the country as in the town. Lonely farms are vulnerable and the wide fertile fields of Holderness and the lonely farms of the Wolds are ideal hunting territory for her gang.

Everyone in the far-flung community fears the sound of many horses in the night and the banging at the door as the gang comes to collect its dues. Mothers threaten their naughty children with her, fathers look over their shoulders on the way to the fields, but what are they to do? The County Militia should be strong enough to deal with Peg and her men, but nothing is ever done and it is said that even they are in her pocket.

How does her gang operate? To begin with a single member will approach you, civilly enough, at the market, perhaps, or in the lane as you drive the cows home for milking. He will remark that your farm is doing well, complimenting you on your hard work. Then he will add something about how easy it is for an unexpected disaster to lose you all that you've worked for, how villains are everywhere, how you need protecting from them. You've got the message by now. Will you pay up? And what will happen if you don't?

There is one farmer near Spurn Point who won't.

'I'll be damned if I give a brass farthing to that foul awd witch. She can go whistle.'

The men who work for him on the farm shake their heads at such dangerous bravado. Still, it's not their brass.

Peg does not take this refusal well. She's no fool; like any Mafia boss she knows that it's fear rather than muscle that keeps the income coming in: she has to act.

Tom, one of the plough lads, is riding his big plough horse out to the fields just before dawn one autumn morning. It promises to be a fine day with a white mist still clinging to the fields. The hedges, tall from the warm summer, arch darkly over, covered with a lace of spiders' webs. There is a rustling in the grass as Bess' big hooves strike down and small creatures run for safety. Tom is happy; he's the first out and it isn't raining. He's singing at the top of his voice.

Suddenly, out of the mist and the black hedges, a figure leaps and grabs Bess' bridle. Bess snorts and backs in alarm, but Tom quiets her. The figure throws back the shawl on its head and a fierce face scowls up at him. At first he thinks it's a man in woman's clothes, it is so hard and weather-beaten. Then he sees the gold rings on the strong fingers and is frozen with fear. The woman laughs.

'Well, my little nightingale, I see you know who I am!'

Tom nods.

'Good. How do they call you?'

'Tom.'

'Now I'm sure you're a right good lad, Tom, so you and me is goin' to do a little business together. I'm goin' to ask you to do summat for me and in return I'll do summat for you.'

'What would you do for me?' asks Tom.

'I'll let you go on breathing, my little cherub. Do we have a bargain?'

Tom is too afraid to argue; he can see the long knife in the hand that isn't holding the bridle. He nods.

'That's me clever lad. Now this is the little thing I need from you: tomorrow night you'll leave the stable door unlocked, do you hear me?'

He nods again.

'And to make sure that you keep your gob shut you're going to swear me a proper oath. Like what lawyers' use, God rot 'em!' She spits on the ground.

'Right, say after me "I promise on my life to leave the stable door unlocked tomorrow night and never to speak a word to a soul about it, s'welp me God and Devil or may I be flayed alive!"'

Tom repeats this with a trembling voice and almost before he has finished Peg has vanished among the hedges, leaving him with 'Remember yer oath Tom!'

Folk in those days held an oath to be much more unbreakable than they do now and Tom is no exception. He's a bright lad, though, and as he guides the plough back and forth behind Bess that day he's wondering how he can foil Peg's plot without breaking his oath. Finally he hits upon what seems like a perfect plan.

That night he begs the farmer to come out to the stables with him as he has something to show him. The famer grumbles but he goes. They stand behind the line of big rumps that stretch away into the darkness, listening to the sound of the clink and rattle of the halter chains and the comfortable chomping of the horses eating their well-earned supper.

'So what's up Tom?' asks the farmer.

'I has summat as I wants to tell the 'osses, Sir,' says Tom. 'Right, you 'osses, listen to me. I've heard a terrible thing. Peg Fyfe is coming to get you and she's made me promise to leave the stable door unlocked tomorrow night. I'll be very sorry to lose you all, specially Bess, but I've sweared a terrible oath not to tell a soul, so as the parson says 'osses have no souls I'm telling you.'

The following night the farmer loads his grandpa's old blunderbuss and waits in the bushes by the stables where Tom has left the door a little ajar. The night is very dark with hardly any moon. Time passes slowly, only the hooting of owls disturbing the silence.

The farmer dozes a little. A rustle wakes him. He stiffens and checks his gun. Dimly in the starlight he sees movement. Black figures are creeping towards the stable.

He stands and calls out 'Who's there?' in a voice of thunder. The figures freeze and then a harsh woman's voice says 'Peg Fyfe!' She is not afraid to announce her presence, relying on the very mention of her name to daunt any challenger. This time the dreaded name fails. The farmer fires in the direction of the voice. A man screams. Loud curses and swearing break out. 'Damn! Missed t'awd bitch!' In the moments of confusion that follow the farmer struggles to reload, but before he can fire again the robbers flee, the wounded man supported by the others. One brave man has driven off Peg Fyfe's gang!

The news spreads across Holderness. Peg's almost mystical hold over the area is destroyed; others begin to stand up to her gang; vigilante groups are formed to protect farms. Some gloomier souls, however, are dubious. 'Peg won't take this lying down. She'll get her revenge, never fear.'

The farmer rewards Tom with money and an old silver medal of his father's which he hangs around his neck on a bit of ribbon. The tale of how 'Tom told the 'osses' is repeated and enjoyed by half the county.

Winter comes and goes but the farmer and his farm are not troubled. It seems that Peg and her gang have left the county. Then, as spring begins to catch fire, Tom doesn't return home one night. The farmer and his people are instantly worried. He's a steady lad, not given to wild escapades. Police have not yet been invented, so they have to make their own inquiries: where was he seen last? Who was he with? They get no answers.

A second night goes by with no sign of him.

In the cold of an early spring morning, with the dawn chorus just getting into full voice, the farmer's wife, up to make bread, hears a muffled banging at the door. She opens it and, at first, sees no one. A movement at her feet makes her glance down. Then her screams bring all the menfolk of the farm rushing into the kitchen, half-dressed.

No longer recognisable, save by the silver medal around its neck, the bloody heap of meat on the doorstep (a hideous heap that gasps and gurgles, steaming in the cold air), stretches out its bony fingers towards them for help.

Peg Fyfe has punished Tom: he has been flayed alive!

REGIN THE FALSE-HEARTED

Nunburnholme
At the tower end of the little church of St James in Nunburnholme, a village at the foot of the Yorkshire Wolds, stand (much to the inconvenience of local bell-ringers) the remains of an ancient cross. It is well known to art historians because it famously combines Christian and pagan images. Crammed on one side under the carving of a bishop is a curious little scene: there is a man holding up his thumb, a couple of what look like doughnuts and, at the bottom, a small hunched figure.

The man is one of the great Scandinavian heroes, Sigurd the Dragon-Slayer, and its inclusion – squeezed in, for some lost reason, after the rest was carved – shows that his story was as well loved and familiar to the eleventh-century people of East Yorkshire as it was to those in Norway or Denmark. It may be that all other Yorkshire dragon stories are its descendants.

There was a young man called Sigurd, just come into his first strength. He lived in the forest with his foster-father, a dwarf smith called Regin. He could not remember his mother, and all he knew of his father was that he had once wielded the broken sword which lay, wrapped in cloth, at the bottom

of the smith's oaken chest. Who his parents had been, or what
had been their tragic story, he did not know, nor would Regin
ever tell him.

As he grew into his power, he also grew restless and bored with
his quiet life. One day an old man appeared at the door of the
hut. He was tall and grey-haired, and the brim of his hat drooped
over his face, almost concealing the empty socket of one eye.

Regin was away, cutting wood for charcoal, so Sigurd
offered the unexpected guest water and food. When they had
talked a while the old man asked Sigurd if he had a horse.
Sigurd shook his head sadly. His foster-father, he said, didn't
believe in wasting money on unnecessary luxuries. The old
man nodded his head slowly. 'It seems a shame that a young
man like you should not have a horse. It just so happens that
I have one that might suit you.' Sigurd explained that he had
no gold to pay for it.

'Never mind. I give him to you in return for your hospitality.
His name is Grani. Treat him kindly for he is the offspring of my
own horse, Sleipnir. He's tethered down there by the birches.'

Sigurd, full of gratitude and excitement, ran down to see.
There, pawing the ground among the pale new birch leaves,
was the most beautiful horse he had ever seen: iron-grey, fiery,
intelligent, strong. A perfect warrior's horse. He ran back to
thank the old man, but he was gone.

When Regin returned home he found Sigurd full of the
story of his horse.

'Now that I have a horse I can ride off to find fame and
fortune. I shall make you proud of me. It is time, my father.
I cannot stay here pulling the bellows arm for you forever!'

The smith looked long and silently at his foster-son and saw,
with something very like fear, that the boy he had found beside
a dying woman all those years ago was indeed fully grown – and
a born warrior, though he still lacked skill and wisdom.

He grunted and turned away. Dwarves have their own dark purposes and it was not out of charity that he had raised the baby.

'Father, you promised me a sword when I was a man. It is time to keep your promise. Make me a sword!'

Regin grumbled; reluctantly he heated his forge. Sigurd took up his usual position at the bellows. The sound of hammer on iron echoed through the spring woods. The sword was made: a fine one, for dwarves are masters of steel. Sigurd took it in his hands and brought it down on the anvil with all his strength. The sword flew into pieces.

'Your sword was too weak, father. Make me a stronger one!'

But that sword broke as well.

Finally, even more reluctantly, the smith took from his chest the fragments of sword that had once belonged to Sigurd's father.

'This was the finest sword ever made,' he said, 'the sword of your father, the great warrior Sigmund. This is a hero's sword. It was only broken because he dared to fight Odin himself. If I can reforge it you must use it as a hero should.'

Long was its forging, but when at last Regin had finished and Sigurd held it in his hands, seeing how the blue-black wave pattern of folded and refolded steel rippled down the blade, he knew it was a sword beyond price. He struck the anvil and clove it in half.

'It is possible that my death is in that sword,' muttered Regin, smiling bitterly but Sigurd did not hear him. 'Now you have such a weapon, my son, I have a task worthy of it – if the hand that wields it is indeed that of a hero!'

Sigurd heard that! 'Tell me!'

'In the mountains there lives a dragon who sleeps on a mound of gold greater than a king's hoard. I will show you where he lives if you will swear to kill him!'

Dwarves have their own dark purposes. Regin did not tell Sigurd that the dragon, Fafnir, was his own brother. Neither did he tell him of the curse that lay on the gold. The origin of that curse lay back deep in time and story, back in the actions of the gods themselves, when the gold had been amassed as wergild [blood-money] for a slain dwarf's son, Regin's other brother, Otter. The gods had stolen the gold to satisfy the vengeful father, but the very last piece, a magic ring, Draupnir, had been cursed by its owner when it was forcibly taken from him.

Gold causes strife enough without an added curse. The brothers Fafnir and Regin soon fell out over the treasure and Fafnir, being the stronger, took it for himself. He hid from Regin in the mountains, becoming a dragon, transformed by greed.

Regin's revenge had taken its time, but it was on its way as Sigurd rode out on Grani the following morning, singing in the clear morning sunshine. Regin shouldered their pack and followed slowly behind.

Mists had risen and obscured the sun by the time they reached the mountains. The two camped some way from the dragon's cave and Regin told Sigurd what he must do.

'Fafnir comes down once a day, in the evening, to drink at that little lake. If you look carefully you can see the smooth track his scraping scales have made. You must dig a pit in that track and hide in it. He will drag his bulk over you unseeing in the dusk and you will be able to stab his unarmoured belly as he passes over you.'

Sigurd would have preferred a proper fight, but he respected Regin's wisdom so he did as he was told. As he was digging he heard a quiet step behind him. He swung around, his hand on his new sword. There stood the old one-eyed man.

'Greetings again, young man. What are you doing?'

'Digging a pit to kill a dragon. I shall stab him as he crawls over me.'

'But what about the blood? Lots of blood in a dragon. It'll make you invulnerable, but that won't be much good if you're drowned.'

'Hm. Strange my foster-father didn't think about that. What should I do?'

'Dig a couple of trenches to drain it off.'

Sigurd thanked him and began digging immediately. He was so busy that he didn't see the old man go away.

Now light was beginning to fade. Regin brought him a hot drink from the camp.

'Good luck, my son. I have no wish to meet Fafnir so I shall be back later to see how things have gone. May your father's sword protect you.'

The mists thickened further as evening drew on. Sigurd hid in his pit with drawn sword. He shivered with excitement, and the wait seemed long and cold, but eventually there came a grating of pebbles, a rasping of rock, a smell of hot iron that reminded him of the forge back home: the dragon was coming. Slowly it came, heaving its vast bulk down the mountain to drink.

Fafnir had slept long on his gold. It had made him stupid, forgetful of danger. Unseeing, he dragged himself over Sigurd's hole. The newly forged sword pierced upwards through his belly, thrust by strong arms, once, twice. The black blood came pouring, steaming down over Sigurd, into the pit and then out into the trenches. With a terrible roar the dragon rolled over and over, coiling in its death agony, smashing trees and bushes as it writhed. Then, with a gurgling cry, it lay still.

Sigurd dragged himself from the pit; his skin was burning with the poisonous blood, but the joy of his first great victory filled his heart. How pleased his foster-father would be! He satisfied himself that the dragon was indeed dead and went to wash himself in the lake. When the blood was all gone his skin gleamed faintly in the darkness: it was now invulnerable, as the old man had said. But heroes, like dragons, all have to have their weak spots; there was a small patch on his back where a leaf had fallen on to it, preventing the blood from touching the skin.

Soon Regin came, lurking and creeping, to see if the dragon had been killed. He jumped violently when he saw Sigurd.

'You are still alive, my son!' he gasped. 'How wonderful! Let us butcher the dragon and eat some of its meat. You, who have proved yourself a hero shall have the flesh. All I want is the heart.'

Sigurd lit a fire while Regin cut some strong green sticks and put great slices of dragon on them to roast. Then he took his spear, stuck the huge dripping heart on to the end and propped it up over the fire. He seemed very tired when he had finished.

'I must sleep, Sigurd. My anxiety for you has worn me out. I shall come back in the morning with a special victory drink for you. Watch the meat and don't let it burn – and please don't forget that the heart is my portion.'

Roasting meat over a fire takes time. The dawn chorus was beginning to sing before it was done. Sigurd turned the slices of dragon to cook them evenly, but the heart cooked more quickly and began to burn. Soon a big blister rose on its surface. As Sigurd reached out to move it further from the heat the blister burst and his thumb was burnt by the hot liquid that sprayed out. He thrust it into his mouth to ease the pain and suddenly a whole chorus of small voices seemed to be speaking all round him. It was the birds, singing, as it seemed to him, in the language of men.

'Sigurd beware!' sang the blackbird.

'Regin is your enemy!' sang the thrush.

'Fafnir was his brother!' sang the chaffinch.

'He raised you only to get the treasure!' sang the blue tit.

'He means to kill you!' sang the robin.

And then, 'He means to kill you!' they all repeated. 'Beware! Beware! Beware!'

Sigurd listened in amazement. Many things that he had not understood about his foster-father began to fall into place. Grief and anger welled up but he could still not completely believe what the birds had said. As the sun rose through the mist he saw his foster-father coming towards him with a cup in his hand.

'Good morning, my hero!' said Regin, with a false smile. 'Here is your victory ale. Drink deep, my son, drink deep!'

'Poison! Poison! Poison!' sang the birds.

Would Sigurd comprehend the complete treachery of his foster-father? As the two stared into each other's eyes, Sigurd glimpsed for the first time the hatred Regin could no longer hide. He made as if to take the proffered drink, then fumbled and dropped it. The spilled liquid frothed and foamed into the green grass, the poison shrivelling it to dust. In another moment, as Regin had foreseen, the blade he had himself forged took its second life, his own.

It was the end of everything Sigurd had ever known. His world swung and teetered as he stood over Regin's body, bloody sword still in hand, horror filling his mind. What should he do? Where should he go?

'Sigurd!' sang the birds, 'The treasure! Take the treasure!'

'Find the beautiful maiden in the fiery circle!

'Find the court of King Giuki!'

'The hero's path, Sigurd. Follow the hero's path!'

Flattered by birds, confused by sorrow, amazement, excitement, ambition, Sigurd left the dragon meat cooking, mounted Grani and set off up the mountain towards the cursed gold and a hero's dark fate.

Notes

1 Animals

How Filey Got its Brig This tale comes from Katherine Briggs'
massive work *Folk Tales of Britain* (London: Routledge and Keegan
Paul, 1974). It was recorded in 1967 from Ruth Tongue. She said
that she got it from 'Young Charley, a Yorkshire under-groom in
Devon'. The usual tale told about Filey Brig is that it was made by
the Devil who dropped his hammer and accidentally picked up a
haddock, gripping it so hard that he caused the spot on its shoulders
known as 'the Devil's Mark'. Seeing his mistake he uttered the
immortal words 'Ha! Dick!' from which the fish gets its name.

The Witch Hare Revd Henderson, *Notes on the Folk-Lore of the
Northern Counties* (London: published for the Folklore Society by
W. Satchell, Peyton & Co.,1879). Variants on this story exist all over
Britain, so it MUST be true …

The Drain Frog From the Norton Collection I: Holderness. The
collection can now be found in the University of Cambridge library.

The Hare and the Prickly Backed Urchin Norton Collection III:
Dialect of Hackness. I have toned down the dialect somewhat. I've
also changed the original moral, which was that you should marry
a woman from your own class because she'd be more like you.

2 THE SEA

Sea Folk   Both this and the following story comes from Peter N. Walker, *Folk Tales from the North York Moors* (London: Robert Hale, 1990).

The Staithes Mermaids   My apologies to the present-day inhabitants of Staithes who, I am sure, would never behave so badly.

Robin Hood Turns Fisherman   This comes from Child Ballad 148A: 'The Noble Fisherman', Francis J. Child, *The English and Scottish Popular Ballads* (Boston and New York: Houghton, Mifflin & Co., 1882–98). Robin Hood's Bay was once just called Bay Town. Its association with Robin Hood (first mentioned in the late sixteenth century) is probably to do with its time-honoured smuggling activities. It seems that Robin's visit to the east coast was followed up by others, this time with the Merry Men, because there are many local wells, stones, etc. named after the outlaw. Peter Walker (in *Folk Tales from the North York Moors*) tells an excellent version of the archery competition between Robin and Little John which is said to be the origin of the Robin Hood and Little John stones near Whitby.

Beggar's Bridge   All the characters in this romantic tale really did exist and the outlines of the story are true. Tom Ferris, whose initials are inscribed on the Beggars' Bridge with the date 1619, did indeed fight against the Armada, become a rich man, marry Agnes and become the Mayor of Hull. The rest is romantic fiction woven, folk-wise, around these facts. Actually the coping stones of the bridge are fourteenth century, so Thomas may have just rebuilt an earlier bridge. He remarried the year after Agnes' death. The strange Russian-looking sheepskin hat that Tom is wearing in the illustration is a copy of those actually worn by Elizabethan sailors. I don't know why it is called Beggars' Bridge, but one suggestion is that, unlike many others, it was toll-free.

The Press Gang   From Revd Thomas Parkinson, *Yorkshire Legends and Traditions* (London: Elliot, Stock, 1889). Fear of the press gang was so common that it even got into folk songs such as 'William Taylor' and 'The Banks of Sweet Dundee'.

3 HOLY FOLK

King Edwin and the Temple of Woden This comes from Bede's *Ecclesiastical History of the English Nation*. The village where Coifi threw the spear is now called Goodmanham. It is one of the oldest settlements in the country and has been inhabited since the Stone Age, probably because of the many springs that rise along the valley. The present church is supposed to be on the site of the great temple to Wotan, though as far as I know it has never been excavated. The whole valley seems to have been a sacred landscape at one time, rather like the Gypsey Race valley. St Helen's Sacred Well, its trees covered with ribbon offerings, is nearby along the old railway line.

Hild and the Snakes Presumably the ammonites found at the foot of the cliffs in Whitby gave rise to this story. There is a collection of really huge ones in the excellent Whitby Museum.

Caedmon Another tale from Bede's *Ecclesiastical History*. Bede says how beautiful Caedmon's Anglo-Saxon was and how difficult it was to translate into Latin. The language of ordinary people wasn't really regarded as respectable enough to be used for serious literature until Chaucer's *Canterbury Tales* 700 years later.

A Miracle Too Far? The Revd Parkinson tells this trickster version of the story – curiously, for a vicar, without comment – in *Yorkshire Legends and Traditions*. Where he got it from is a mystery, but it is obviously a post-Catholic version of Bede's original story, probably eighteenth century, containing the usual Protestant sneers at miracles and monks. The tale (minus Wulfstan and Godruff) comes from Bede's particularly vivid account of St John's miracles, where he recounts things told to him by people who had actually met the saint and been present at the miraculous events. St John (not to be confused with the St John in the Bible) is also credited with having appeared to help the English at the Battle of Agincourt and there are several holy wells dedicated to him. The '*fridstol*' (peace stool), said to be St John's bishop's chair, stands now by the altar in Beverley Minster. It was once possible (until Henry VIII meanly stopped the practice) to claim sanctuary by sitting in it. Having claimed sanctuary you were able to go freely anywhere within a mile of the minster for forty days without being harmed or arrested by your enemies. At the end of that time you had two options: either face trial by the authorities for whatever you were accused of, or walk, with your head shaved, following a specified route, in a specified number of days, to the nearest port to take ship for exile abroad. Should you just do a runner then you were in danger of serious retribution – if caught. The effect of having lots of dubious criminals lounging about town can be imagined, so I don't suppose the inhabitants of Beverley missed the ancient custom much.

4 ODDITIES

Good Vittles   Addy, 'Four Yorkshire Folk Tales', in Folklore VIII, Norton Collection. The information about the hiring fair and the verses from 'Mutton Pies' come from Dr Charles Kightly's *Country Voices: Life and Lore in Farm and Village* (London: Thames and Hudson, *c*.1984), which records interviews with some of the last of the pre-war generation of farmers and their wives.

Saltersgate Inn   You can find many versions of this story on the Internet. Saltersgate was the name of the road (gate = road) by which salt, vital for preserving, was transported from the coast for sale inland. The inn really was a coaching inn, suitably (if predictably) called the Coach and Horses until fairly recently. Smuggling was regarded as a legitimate career in the eighteenth century on the east coast, where the imposition of taxes was thought an insult to all independently minded persons, male or female. A rival tale says that the fire was kept alight either to hide the dead body of a murdered Excise man, or to prevent his ghost from walking. A curious feature of this story is that the fire is used to trap the Devil, whereas anyone at all familiar with folklore knows that fires are traditionally lit to keep *away* demons, etc.

The Flying Man   From Alexandra Medcalf:
www.borthwickinstitute.blogspot.co.uk.

The White Powder   From *County Folklore*, Vol. 6, collected and edited
by Mrs Gutch (London: David Nutt, 1912) It has been suggested that
the fairy mound was Willey Howe near Wold Newton.

Village Stereotypes   From Gutch, *County Folklore*, Vol. 6.

5 THE OTHER SIDE

The Baby in a Shoe   Midwives did indeed have the right to christen
babies if there was a danger of them dying. This was because
men, including priests, were not allowed in the birthing room.
An unbaptised baby could not be buried in the graveyard and would
not go straight to Heaven, but to Limbo, a boring place invented by
theologians to comfort mothers and resolve various thorny problems
about original sin from which even newborns were supposed to suffer.

The Tailor and the Wayside Ghost   Like the story above, this story
was discovered by M.R. James and published untranslated in
Latin. This translation is by Pamela Chamberlaine and I found it
in *M.R. James: Book of the Supernatural*, edited by Peter Haining
(Slough: W. Foulsham & Co. Ltd, 1979).

The Three Roses   This sinister little tale comes from William Hone's
The Table Book, Vol. 2 (London: Thomas Tegg, 1841).

Five White Pebbles   Various sources including Katherine Briggs,
Folk Tales of Britain, Vol. 3.

The Fairy Cup   William of Newburgh tells this story in his twelfth-
century *Historia rerum Anglicarum*.

The Screaming Skull   This story is well-known locally and can be found
in many sources. There is a picture reputed to be of the three sisters in
the house, which is open to the public. You'll have to ask the present
owner, Simon Cunliffe-Lister, about the skull. There is often a hint
in Yorkshire folklore that the dead can come back as disturbing hobs

or boggarts. 'Awd Nance's' activities sound remarkably like those of a boggart. Screaming isn't as unusual a behaviour for skulls as you might think. There are quite a few others around the country, all with their own curious stories.

Jeannie o' Biggersdale   Peter N. Walker, *Folk Tales from the North York Moors*. Cutting a horse in half as it leaps across water appears to be a common practice of witches – in fact it's also in one version of 'The Fairy Cup'.

The Drumming Well   Revd Parkinson, *Yorkshire Legends and Traditions*. The actual well is near the church and surrounded with an iron railing – presumably to stop the drummer acquiring a spectral group.

6 VILLAINY

The Babe in the Wood   This dastardly story comes from a highly dubious ballad given a gloss of truth by the use of such phrases as 'about two years ago' and 'The Assizes being held on Monday last'. It is quoted in Gutch, *County Folklore*, Vol. 6, where it is recorded as having been originally published as 'The Distressed Child in the Wood' or 'The Cruel Uncle' published by J. Read behind the Green Dragon Tavern in Fleet Street, London (1706). What its influence may have had on the traditional 'Babes in the Wood' pantomime story, which it predates, I'm not sure. As in our modern version (and unlike the Victorian one, which is a real tear-jerker) the babe does not die!

The Penny Hedge   H.L. Gee, *Folk Tales of Yorkshire* (London and Edinburgh: Thomas Nelson and Sons Ltd, 1952). As this story illustrates, many old customs come, not from ancient Celtic religions, but from the much more unromantic need to establish land ownership and boundaries. Exactly what was being established here by the Horngarth is not clear, but probably has to do with the rights of the townsfolk vis-à-vis the abbey, which owned most of the land.

Fishgarths (fish traps) were commonly built along rivers to catch eels and fish so it may be that building one every year established the townsfolk's rights to fish the Esk – but this is just speculation. The date usually given for the killing of the hermit is 1159 – but on what authority I know not. You can see the Horngarth or Penny Hedge Ceremony every year at 9 a.m. on the eve of Ascension Day. It takes place in Whitby's upper harbour on the east bank of the River Esk.

The Milking Stool/Peggy Flaunders From Blakeborough, *Wit, Character, Folklore and Customs of the North Riding of Yorkshire* (London: Henry Frowde, 1898). Injury to beasts by witchcraft and the stealing of milk seems to have been a particular obsession in the past and this is just one tale of many.

The Hand of Glory All three Yorkshire versions of this story are given in Katherine Briggs, *Folk Tales of Britain*.

Cruel Peg Fyfe John Nicholson, *Folklore of East Yorkshire* (London: Simpkin, Marshal, Hamilton, Kent & Co., 1890). Peg was probably a real person, now claimed as an inhabitant by Market Weighton. She is also supposed to have been a witch – no surprises there! Her nasty career seems to have ended with her being hanged; according to one version she swallowed a spoon in order to cheat the noose but it didn't work. Her latest incarnation is as a dark mild beer of the same name, brewed at the Goodmanham pub.

Regin the False-Hearted This story is part of a much longer tale. It has been told in different versions for at least 1,000 years. The best known is probably Wagner's 'Siegfried', the third of his operas in *The Ring of the Nibelungs* cycle. The cursed ring is, of course, going to be the cause of Sigurd's death.